DANGEROUS FLAME

January Kelly

CONTENTS

ALSO BY

Paranormal Romantic Suspense
The Hidden Series:
The Night They Knew- a short story from The Hidden
Hidden Intent
Smoke and Shadow
Relative Deceit
Standalone:
The Last Lament of the Late Shawn Reilly
Contemporary Fiction
All These Days

www.januarykelly.com

Follow on Facebook:

https://www.facebook.com/profile.php?id=100067850730415

Instagram:

https://www.instagram.com/januarykelly.author/?next=%2F

For Mom

I think this would be her jam.

ACKNOWLEDGEMENTS

I am so lucky to have in my life a wonderful husband who never shows jealousy when the characters in my books get more of my attention than he does. I only wish every person could have a partner like I was fortunate enough to find. He, along with our children, makes being a writer a little easier...especially when someone else does the dishes.

My stories would not be half as good as they are without the tireless efforts of my editor Kymmee. Your hard work and ineffable mind are beyond measure and something I cannot live without. You are a fiery talent with words of wisdom and questions that always cause my brain to expand like the galaxies. May you conquer the universe in the steps of Calliope, Minerva, and Brigid.

I want to recognize and thank my partner in book crime, Amanda for all of her encouragement, late-night brainstorming texts, and validation that the existence of imposter syndrome is a real thing and we all have it. You, my friend, are incredible and I appreciate your existence on my journey. Everyone should consume your brilliant art, devouring the worlds you create and find themselves in your magic. I wish you every success this universe holds.

There are so many more behind the scenes that keep me going and I know I will never do them justice. For Church, my very first Beta reader; Sarah, my longest friend; Robin, my biggest fan, and Missy, my de-facto "fan club" President...THANK YOU FROM THE BOTTOM OF MY HEART.

The playlist that entertained in the creative venture of this book:

Ordinary World- Duran Duran

Right Here Right Now- Jesus Jones

Summer of '69- Bryan Adams

Fade Into You- Mazzy Star

Black- Pearl Jam

Everybody Hurts- R.E.M

This Used To Be My Playground- Madonna

Please Forgive Me- Bryan Adams

Leave A Light On- Papa Roach

Cry Little Sister- Gerard Mcmann

Pride, envy, avarice- these are the sparks have set
on fire the hearts of all men. — Dante Alighieri

CHAPTER ONE

CHARLIE

I pulled my rental car into a parking space in front of the Hilton on Parkway Avenue. I decided against staying at the same hotel as the reunion because if I needed to make a quick exit, it might be in my best interest to make a clean getaway. I really had no desire to get stuck in a conversation with someone on an elevator or hallway the following morning. I'm not a snob, I just didn't want to answer a million questions about what I had been doing the past twenty or so years or see their look of pity when "I'm sorry about your parents" fell from their mouths.

Again.

My mom and dad, Claire and Jasper, were well-known and well-loved in our little community on the far outskirts of Portland. My father was the high school biology teacher and soccer coach and my mother was what they called a homemaker. In reality, she was an accountant-taxi-chef-seamstress-PTA president-extraordinaire. They lived healthy, happy, average, lives and weren't the kind of people that one would expect tragedy to hit. When a tractor-trailer crossed the center line on a curved stretch of Wilsonview Road though, that apple pie life was over for them and me.

Now, I sat staring at the seven-story white building in front of me and reconsidered my commitment to going inside. I hadn't seen any of these people in at least twenty years, and I was certain I wouldn't recognize most of them. This was stupid. I'm a goddamn federal agent, why am I bothering with a high school reunion, for God's sake?

Because I had the time off and nothing else to do, that's why.

"Charlie, you've got the time to take...do it before I make it an order."

Bart Covey, Deputy Special Agent in Charge, and my direct boss, told me in his office a week ago.

I didn't argue. My last case was a rough one, most of them were, but this one was especially disgusting. My team worked it for the better part of a long, exhausting, year. A child sex ring where the leader was a father of three daughters that he pimped out to his child molesting buddies. The children ranged in age from twelve to sixteen. This guy had no scruples and even sold a nine-year-old boy to a pedophile. Believe me when I say, there is no amount of time at the gym, shooting range, or in a bar that can wipe away those images. They made my skin crawl.

"I don't want to see you for the next ten days. Is that understood?"

Covey ordered me in his not-so-indirect way.

So after some thought, I finally decided on a road trip home for a few days. But now, sitting in the parking lot of the Hilton, I reconsidered my decision-making process. At first, I stupidly thought it might be fun to kick around my old stomping grounds and have a quick visit with some family that I hadn't seen in more than a decade. To my surprise, things had changed drastically as Hydrangea Falls was no longer the sleepy little farming community on the edges of Portland. Like most of the other towns in the area, innovation, and urban sprawl crept to its edges, bringing with it money, people, and likely, crime.

Everything led to that it seemed. Usually does.

But, the Falls, as we locals referred to it, still has its charm. The downtown square is still homey and quaint in appearance with the large white courthouse at its center. While most of the old businesses I would recognize no longer existed, I was happy to see that new owners were renovating the classic buildings and bringing new life to Main Street. It was when I parked in front of the Rexall Pharmacy that my plans for a low-key visit were diverted. The familiar bell rang over my head as I pulled on the glass door to walk inside and mom's sister, my Aunt Nettie, stared at me over her wire-rimmed glasses.

"Well...I'll be damned. Charlotte Ann...is that you?" Nettie's full cheeks spread into a wide smile.

"Hi, Aunt Nettie," I walked to the counter as she came around it. Throwing her chubby arms around me, she pulled me in tightly to her large bosom.

"Well, I never...why didn't you tell us you was gonna be here? Did ya come for the reunion?" she asked, kissing me on the cheek.

I stared at her a moment. Time seemed to come to a halt on her face. She looked exactly the way I remembered. "What reunion?"

Nettie seemed genuinely shocked.

"Well...Wildcats class of 1993 is having their reunion over at that big hotel on Parkway tomorrow night. Didn't cha get the invite? I think I saw it on that Facebook or somethin'," she replied.

I laughed to myself. I found it hysterical that my eighty-year-old aunt was using social media and I didn't. And it's not because I didn't know how but that I just didn't want to. I dealt with it enough in my career as an investigative tool; no way I would let someone use it on me. I'm perfectly fine connecting the old-fashioned way—by text message.

"I don't know, Nettie...I'm not sure I'm the reunion type of woman," I shrugged.

She eyed me, "Now...don't tell me you went and got uppity and too good for your old friends, Miss FBI."

'Ouch...that was harsh,' my mind whispered softly.

My aunt was nothing if not direct. But maybe the old woman was right since I *did* come back to visit family. What would it hurt to stop in and see some old friends?

"You're right, Aunt Nettie. Maybe it would be nice to visit with some familiar faces," I smiled.

Turning to resume her post behind the counter, one that she had held for nearly fifty years, Nettie smiled, "That's better...and don't worry...Davy won't be there. He's done got himself locked up again. Stealing copper or somethin' this time."

"And grand theft auto," I gave her a pained smile. "Yeah, I make sure I know where he is."

I hated talking about my idiot ex-husband. Biggest mistake ever. But, what did anyone expect out of a moon-eyed eighteen-year-old?

Nettie nodded, "Yeah...that's probably smart. Sugar...I'd better get back to pricing these new figurines. We're already gettin' stuff in for Christmas. You come by Sunday after church and have lunch, okay?"

Nodding, I replied, "Alright...I'll see you Sunday...as long as you're making fried chicken."

The old woman howled with laughter, "Baby...you heard me right? I did say Sunday lunch."

God, I've really missed her.

Chapter Two

CHARLIE

"Here goes nothing," whispering to myself, I stepped out of the black sedan.

My stiletto heels clicked loudly as I walked across the blacktop of the expansive parking lot. I smoothed out my ultra-professional black pants suit before adjusting my thin purse over my shoulder. As I came closer to the doors, I looked one last time at my reflection. My dark hair pulled back into a ponytail at the base of my neck was neat and tidy showing off my tiny silver hoops glittering in the setting sun. I wondered if I was wearing too much makeup. I couldn't tell in the glass, but why would it matter? I hadn't seen any of these people in years, it would be like meeting all new friends anyway. I took a deep breath and opened the door.

A muffled song by Jesus Jones and a blast of cold, filtered air hit me like a wall.

I took another deep breath and, after finding my name tag on the unmanned folding table just outside the conference room doors, I pushed open the large wooden behemoths and made my way into the darkened, crowded room. I stood just inside the entrance momentarily, taking in the scene.

Around thirty round tables were arranged neatly throughout the spacious room. Each table was covered in black cloth with large gold and black balloon centerpieces. On the far left wall, a small stage was set with a deejay and a light system flashing to the beat of the current song playing, something by Duran Duran, over the sound system. At the opposite end of the room, a buffet table looked to be covered with a large assortment of finger foods and a long line of guests. I turned to my immediate right and found the closest bar.

"Light beer, please," I asked the young bartender as I gave him a ten-dollar bill. After handing me the glass of amber liquid, I told the man, "Keep the change."

Sticking to the edges of the throngs of people, I sipped on my drink and observed. It's something I'm exceptionally good at doing. I tried to get just close enough that I could read individual name tags in hopes I could start a conversation with someone because, after this long, the faces of youth morphed with time, age, and worry.

"Charlie Hanson...is that you?" a voice behind me asked excitedly.

I turned around quickly to find a short, plump, blonde woman staring up at me. Her brilliant blue eyes sparkled behind dark-rimmed glasses. She wore a bright pink dress of some sort of flowy fabric with matching high heels that looked like they came out of a comic book. A wave of regret washed over me as

I finally recognized someone. I would know those eyes and that round face in any situation, in any city, in any country, on any planet.

Jesus. This was going to be a long night.

"Audrey Campbell?" I forced a grin.

Audrey giggled wildly as she threw her arms around me awkwardly, "Oh my God! It's so good to see you! It's actually Audrey Dawson now."

She threw her hand in my face to show me the gaudiest diamond ring I'd ever seen.

"I've missed you! I had no idea you were coming," her gigantic smile stretched from ear to ear.

I shrugged, "Neither did I."

The comment drew a look of confusion, but the overly happy woman shook it off quickly. She turned to a balding man next to her, tugging on his blue polo shirt.

"Jimmy! I want to introduce you to someone," she squealed. "This was my very best friend, back in the day, as they say...Charlie Hanson. Charlie, this is my husband, Jimmy Dawson.

Reaching out, I shook Jimmy's hand.

"Good to meet you," Jimmy said matching his wife's cheerfulness. "What kind of work you do?"

I took a sip of beer, nodding. Jimmy gets right to the point.

"Law enforcement," I swallowed.

"Ooo...that must be exciting," Audrey feigned an eerie voice.

I wanted to vomit.

"Paperwork mostly...and bad coffee," I downplayed. I enjoy my job and love putting bad people in jail, but talking about the dirty details of my career was something I liked to avoid. Mainly because what I do doesn't make for the greatest topic of conversation and causes other people to be uncomfortable. A fact I understand, to an extent. Most people know someone who chose police work, but not someone who continued to climb like I had. And, with my rocky past, no one would've imagined *I* was the same person.

Jimmy, his wide forehead wrinkled in thought, eyed me for a moment. He reminded me of a used car salesman. Someone who uses finger guns and pops gum between his overly bleached teeth.

"Desk work, huh?" Shaking his head as if he felt sorry for me, "I hear police work is rough...especially for women. Ah, well...maybe it's time to enjoy your husband and kids."

There it was. The classic assumption was that I was nothing more than a meter maid or a secretary who spent her days typing memos and getting coffee for the men.

I didn't react the way I wanted to. That would have entailed sweeping his legs, taking him to the ground, and handcuffing his greasy ass. What a misogynistic, knuckle-dragging ape. I could only imagine what my team would have said at this moment. My partner, Jack Brent, would probably sit back, sell tickets to the show, and laugh as he guzzled the popcorn.

Instead, I smiled sweetly at the couple, "Once divorced, too many years ago to count. Audrey can tell you about that. No kids...and there isn't a lot of time for domesticity when you're arresting murderers and child rapists for the FBI."

Audrey and Jimmy stared at me, mouths agape. That was the reaction I was going for.

"It was so nice seeing you, Audrey. I'm gonna check out the buffet," I smiled once more for effect, tipping my beer in their direction. I turned quickly and wove through a small group of women, I'm pretty sure were also former cheerleaders, like Audrey, who were laughing and talking excitedly.

When I thought I was far enough away, and not quite near the tables of food, I meandered to a spot near another bar to people-watch. I just decided to introduce myself to different small group standing nearby when a very tall, handsomely fa-miliar man walked in front of me and stopped. He looked over his broad shoulder and smiled a bright grin that nearly encom-passed his entire face. He stared at me for a long, uncomfortable moment.

"Charlie Hanson. I'll be damned," the man said in a smooth, deep voice that sent a pleasurable chill up my spine.

Tilting my head, I concentrated hard on that voice, "Eric?"

His face lit up once again and he wrapped his arms around me, swallowing me in his embrace.

"How have you been?" he asked excitedly.

Now this *was* a pleasant surprise. Eric Tilset and I were next-door neighbors as children if it could be called that. The Tilset farm and the ten acres my family occupied ran parallel to each other, only separated by Deep Bow Creek. I instantly remembered hot summer days spent in the ice-cold water of the spring-fed creek, catching crawdads for fishing with the Tilset boys. Back then, Eric was a scrawny kid with sharp features and a head too big for his body. He had certainly changed, in the most pleasing way possible.

I returned his hug, "I'm...good. And you?"

Releasing me, Eric stepped back smiling, "I'm well...I had no idea you were coming. Are you staying long?"

I stared in amazement. Time had only been good to Eric. I could tell, through his relatively expensive suit, that he took very good care of himself and was pleased to see he grew out of his childhood lankiness. He really was a bean pole in his younger years. His dark hair was cut short along the sides with the longer portion on top combed back. He was clean-shaven, and when he smiled his mossy, dark eyes sparkled.

"No...not long. I had a little time off work...thought I would visit Aunt Nettie and Josie. I actually didn't know this was happening until Nettie told me," I replied.

He pointed at my near-empty glass, "Let me buy you another beer...we can find a table and talk. It's been a long time."

Chapter Three

CHARLIE

While I would hardly like to admit it, growing up in a place like Hydrangea Falls had its advantages. Childhood memories seem sunnier and idealistic. Neighbors knew and most likely, spent time with each other. Even for a kid like me, who grew up just outside of the Falls, knowing friendly faces was easy because they were all that way. And if I had to count how many close friends I had back then, Audrey and Eric would easily break the top ten.

Until high school, Audrey and I were like peas in a pod. She, the petite child with curly blonde pigtails, dazzling blue eyes, and a bubbly personality was my perfectly matched opposite. She enjoyed talking, playing with dolls, daydreaming, and giggling far more than my reading of books and adventuring in the woods. She is upbeat and cheery and I am always a little more cautious and in my own head. I am the dark and she is the light.

When I wasn't with my number one gal pal, I could always be found on the bank of Bow Bend Creek watching all three Tilset boys fishing and playing in its clear water. Eric was always looking to escape the torment of his older brothers, so we would break away to catch crayfish or frogs further upstream or climb trees in the small wooded patch on my side of the water.

My favorite time of year back home was always summer because even though there was no school, my days were still jam-packed. Long days of swimming in the creek or nearby lake, plenty of fishing, and late nights catching lightning bugs with Eric. There were also endless nights of sleepovers with Audrey. Since Aunt Nettie ran the vacation bible school program at our church, we were even allowed to stay with her for the entire week at her home where we could eat and drink all the junk food and soda our stomachs could hold.

Church was always a large part of my life as a child. My parents weren't particularly religious, but they felt it couldn't do any harm. After all, that's where a person's moral compass is usually forged. And in a small town like the Falls, most everyone went to church on Sunday. Afterward, we'd end up at Aunt Nettie and Uncle Bill's for fried chicken, mashed potatoes, rolls, and pie. In retrospect, maybe I grew up in Mayberry.

Seeing Audrey and now Eric brought back a flood of those memories. I never really thought about my childhood, at least, not since my parents died in a car accident ten years ago. Thinking about the Falls felt painful, and that pain wasn't something I had time for in my life.

Chapter Four

ERIC

"Thanks," Charlie smiled as I pulled out the chair for her. We sat with our drinks on a table in the far corner overlooking the wide room.

I took a sip from my drink, "You talked to anyone else tonight? I mean, I don't recognize half of these people."

"My God! I thought it was just me," Charlie laughed. "Although I did have a nice hello with Audrey Campbell...excuse me, *Audrey Dawson*, earlier."

"Oh yeah? Audrey Campbell huh? How'd that go?" I smirked because I knew it would be a tense reunion. But, I didn't see the police anywhere, so Charlie clearly didn't punch her.

"I'm not saying it was awkward...but," Charlie took a pull of her beer.

"Isn't she the one that tried to steal Davy away from you?" I asked slyly.

Yeah, I knew the answer. Was it a kind of a dick comment? Yeah, but I know Charlie; well, *knew* her. Surely she still had a sense of humor. She narrowed her hazel eyes on me. I was being cheeky, and she saw right through me. Some things didn't change with time.

She pursed her lips, "Hindsight. I should have given him to her."

I pulled a hissing sound through my teeth.

"Still sore about that, huh? Sorry to bring it up," I apologized sincerely.

Grinning, Charlie shook her head, "Hell no, just a mistake that I'd like to go away."

"Ever make that mistake again?" the corner of my mouth spread in a devious grin. God, I always loved to tease this girl. We had been so close as children and even as young teens, we had a connection that even we didn't understand. I was honestly relieved to see her.

"Are you asking if I'm married?" she giggled. "Smooth."

Roaring with laughter, I shrugged, "I mean...we're just catching up, that's all.

"No, not married," she replied with a chuckle."I think once was enough."

"Me either," I stated flatly, playing with my glass. What I didn't say was I had never come close to marriage, but I was betting money, even though she denied it now, she had again.

A long pause fell between us and we people watched for a few moments, listening to the music of our youth. I couldn't remember the last time I had seen Charlie. At her parent's funeral, maybe? That would've been almost a decade now and I know I didn't talk to her back then. She looked good. Damn good. A small group of women walked by slowly and waved at me.

Jesus...I hope I didn't sleep with any of you...

I returned the gesture in kind before taking another sip of beer and continuing my wallow in self-deprecation.

"So, what are you doing now?" Charlie asked as the switch between songs created a welcome lull in the noise level.

"I'm a firefighter...out in Las Vegas," I replied.

Charlie's eyes widened, "Wow, I had no idea. That's fantastic! How long have you lived there?"

"Close to eighteen years now, you?" I took a drink from my glass and watched the silky remnants of suds sliding down the side and collecting at the bottom.

Charlie sighed and I thought for a second that it was a weird reaction. I knew what she did for a living and I knew why she never visited this place. Too many bad memories, and that I understood. But, my parents were still alive and living on their farm. It was easier to just have an aunt and cousin as your only connection. When your parents still were around, not coming back wasn't exactly an option.

"Oh," Charlie shrugged, "After I divorced Davy, I finally got my life together. Ended up working in Denver...then on to Virginia. I'm living in Seattle right now."

"FBI life seems exciting," I smirked from behind my glass.

A grin spread across Charlie's face and I thought I saw a small glint of relief cross her eyes. I assumed she'd want to tell people all about her life, it actually surprised me that she didn't.

"Looks like I'm not the only investigator here," she laughed.

I sat my empty glass down, chuckling, "No...just...unlike you, I come around a little more often than every generation or so. Nettie was pretty proud when you were accepted at Quantico."

"She...was?" Charlie's nose wrinkled in disbelief.

"Told everyone that would listen...which is a lot of people, considering she knows every family in a thirty-mile radius," I laughed, leaning on the table. "I assume you're still working for them?"

Charlie nodded, "Yeah...it's kinda why I'm here. Orders."

I raised my eyebrows at her. *This* would be classic Charlie and I wondered what kind of trouble she got herself into now.

"Someone *forced* you to take a vacation?" I asked.

"Something like that," she shrugged.

A deep quiet fell between us again and was a stark contrast to the music that thundered around us. Charlie noticed my empty glass and offered to get me another.

"I'm good...two is my limit," I smiled at her. "I tend to get into trouble beyond that."

Pulling out a pack of gum, I unwrapped the red stick and folded it into my mouth. I started bending the wrapper deftly between my fingertips. Charlie couldn't tell what I was doing, as she watched my hands, but I continued to bend and twist the paper without explanation. The music in the room changed to a soft, rock ballad and I looked over to her.

"Would you want to dance?" I asked a little nervously.

She seemed to be considering her options. If she was anything like me, she really didn't want to be here at all. Other than my parents, I turned my back on everyone in Hydrangea Falls. The sleepy little town wasn't for me anymore, if it even was back then. I had broken too many hearts and burned too many bridges. I was honestly lucky there wasn't anyone carrying pitchforks and demanding my hanging at this party. I rose from my seat and placed my hand out to her. "Well?"

Charlie slid her soft fingers into mine and I guided her to the dance floor.

CHAPTER FIVE

CHARLIE

Eric slid his arm around my waist, pulling me close to his chest. From this angle, I had to tilt back to see his dark green eyes. His grasp around me was strong and I felt a sense of safety in it. As I held onto his shoulders, I could feel the well-formed muscles that were snug under his shirt and jacket. But, it made sense to me, he was a firefighter, after all. His cologne smelled fresh like pine needles and ocean mist in my nose. I quite liked the scent and leaning closer, I discreetly filled my nostrils with it. I suddenly realized my heart was racing as we drifted over the dance floor. It surprised me that I felt this attracted to someone I'd known my whole life.

But I shouldn't be *that* surprised.

Since our freshmen year of high school, I knew Eric had a crush on me. He never knew it, but the feelings were definite-ly reciprocated. We were like two ships passing in the night, though. Every time we seemed to make progress, a storm would come along and throw us off course. The last hurricane was Davy.

Back in high school, I was just another small-town girl waiting for the right guy to come along and sweep me off my feet. Unfortunately, all I found was Davy Wyatt. He was dangerously cute, smoked Marlboro reds, and drove a black Trans Am. At the time, stars and hormones filled my eyes and I only had thoughts for the local bad boy. We had a complicated and often messy relationship filled with break-ups and make-ups. On graduation night, Davy drunkenly proposed to me, after which we were married a month later at the Multnomah County courthouse.

Married life didn't change much for us as a couple. While at first, all of our past ups and downs seemed to iron themselves out, it only took eight months for Davy to resume his partying lifestyle. I wanted commitment and partnership; Davy wanted to fix cars and drink all night with his buddies. While I worked two part-time jobs to keep the bills paid in our tiny three-room apartment, Davy slept off hangovers. Everything came to a head when, after working for nearly fifteen hours a day, every day, I came home to find Audrey Campbell passed out half-naked on my sofa.

After promptly throwing the woman out of my house along with my husband, I took what little money I could save and filed for divorce. Embarrassed and heartbroken, I moved in with friends in Portland and enrolled in college. After earning my bachelor's degree in Psychology, I moved to Denver for work. But unsatisfied with my nine-to-five office job, I decided to make an even more drastic change. I applied for and was accepted into the police academy. After five years as a patrolman with an outstanding record, I took the leap, and the test, to advance into the homicide division as a detective. A few years after that promotion, I could hear the FBI calling my name.

Looking down into my eyes as we swayed, Eric cleared his throat, "So, I have a confession to make."

"Oh, yeah? What's that?" I asked, amused.

"I...uhhh...I kinda had a crush on you...you know, back then," he admitted.

Choking a giggle, I replied, "Really?"

Eric smiled with his entire face, "I did. I never knew if you knew that, or not."

"Nope...not at all," I shook my head, lying. "Why didn't you ever ask me out?"

Eric threw his head back in laughter, "I'm not sure you would've said yes...I wasn't going to take that chance."

I shrugged, "That's fair."

A second song began and we continued our dance, only stopping when we recognized old friends who were within range to chat. I found myself in open laughter more than once as we retold old stories of our collective misspent youth.

"Do you remember the Fourth of July and the bottle rocket...*incident*?" Eric stifled a laugh.

"Oh? That's what you're calling it? The incident?" I looked at him with raised brows and humorous disbelief.

We continued our gentle swaying to the music.

His face lit up, beaming, "I mean...what would you call it?"

"Oh, you mean when a group of sixteen-year-olds near-ly burned a field down because they decided that binding together one hundred and fifty bottle rockets...and lighting them...would be a great idea? Probably misdemeanor arson," I replied, snickering.

Laughing, Eric continued to twirl me, "More like a felony...and lucky because none of us were hurt."

"You're dad was so pissed," I giggled remembering Dec Tilset's red face as he ran with his garden hose toward the fire.

"Not as much as my mother," he grinned, "It was her prized rose bush we ruined."

Until I bumped into Eric, this night was clearly going to be a mistake. But, in the last hour, I noticed I enjoyed myself more than I had in the last year. For the first time since I landed, I was forgetting everything about my recent case and the past six months.

Eric is beautifully handsome. Maybe it was the situation and the ambiance that was being created, but he was familiar and comforting; feelings that I hadn't felt or found in quite a long time. But I also felt off balance with him. He was the first man in a very long time that excited me and it threw me into a spin. If he could read my thoughts, I'd be embarrassed and would probably break out into a full-body blush because I was imagining what he looked like under that navy suit.

Naked. What did he look like naked?

Jesus Christ, Charlie.

My thoughts roared in my mind.

"How's the family?" I asked as his strong arms guided me across the floor. I had to get my mind on something else. Anything but how good those arms felt around my waist.

Eric shrugged nonchalantly, "Pop is good...mom's always giving him a hard time. They're still out at the farm. Billy's still around...he and his wife just had their first grandkid. Colby's had the same boyfriend since college. They live in San Diego."

"I haven't seen your brothers in years," I smiled. Being an only child, I always looked at the older Tilset boys as if they were my own brothers. They seemed to always see me in the same regard and never treated me any differently than Eric when we were children.

Another song changed, and we continued to sway to the music in pregnant silence for a moment.

"I gotta say, the music really sets a mood," I chuckled nervously.

Eric smiled down at me, "Yeah, this deejay is a time traveler. It's like being back at our senior prom."

There was a memory unlocked—senior prom.

I was dressed in a slim maroon sequin, white taffeta mermaid flared dress and the theme was *Kiss From A Rose* as Whitney Houston bellowed over the speakers. My full memory of that night was hazy, but I saw the picture of Davy and me the photographer had taken when we arrived as if it were branded in my brain. Luckily, what no one noticed in that photo were the red blotches under my eyes where I had been crying not thirty minutes before. Just another one of our infamous break-ups and make-ups.

Luckily for me, crisp spring air and Cover Girl powder hid my tear-streaked face.

"Penny for your thoughts?" Eric's deep voice snapped me back to reality.

Shaking my head, I smiled, "Nothing...just thinking how this night is already better than that prom."

He smiled back, nodding.

The later the evening became, the more my thoughts ran a million beats a second in my mind. I had to get myself together because this wasn't like me. The music changed again and Mazzy Star played over the air.

Then again, it had been a very long time since I had been with anyone. But the more Eric and I spoke, the stronger the connection I felt. My heart delightfully fluttered like a schoolgirl but it irritated and annoyed me at the same time. I suddenly felt his body tense as his massive arms pulled me into him. Leaning down close, he whispered in my ear.

"It was nice seeing you again, Charlie. I think I'd better be going," his deep voice breathed. His tenor sent chills through me that made my knees weak.

What the hell is wrong with me?

Also, those were not the words I expected. With one last squeeze of my hand, he walked off the dance floor as the song reached its climax.

I stood in disbelief for a moment. What the hell just happened? I watched him meander through small, dwindling groups of people who were chatting their way through last-call cocktails until he reached the large wooden door and walked out. I had never been left in a greater state of shock. No way was I going to let him leave without an explanation, so I followed him. I lost sight of him until I walked out of the automated glass doors of the hotel and caught his tall frame making its way to the corner of the lot.

"Hey!" I called.

He seemed to ignore me, so I moved faster. I wanted to catch up to him before he could get in his car and leave. Now, I was more determined than ever to get an answer. An answer for what, I didn't know. Maybe for why he left so suddenly. I was practically running now and didn't realize the figure I was headed for was stopped, waiting for me to catch up.

"Hey!" I called again as I came to the edge of his sedan, pulling in a deep breath of spring night air, "Why'd you leave?"

Eric, who already slid out of his sport coat, was pulling off his tie when he turned to me. This time when he looked at me, his face seemed pained.

"Because I have to."

I watched his jaw clench and release as his eyes studied my face. I was on guard, but no more than I normally was, but I did realize he was completely shutting down. His energy shifted oddly, but I didn't feel danger from him or that he was a threat. I was so confused.

"What the hell, Eric? I thought we were having a good time—" I said before he cut me off.

He hung his head, "I've probably had a better time with you tonight than with anyone in a very long time. But...this is all fake, Charlie. It's been great catching up with you...but, I don't want to do anything I'm going to regret. I know where this leads, and I'm not that guy anymore. So, I'm going back to my hotel room...*alone*...getting up tomorrow and going back to Vegas. And now, you'll do the same. No regrets and we can still be friends."

I was speechless. I appreciated the chivalry, but not having my choices made for me. It was all so damn confusing.

"I hope we can see each other again...if you're ever in Vegas," leaning down, he wrapped his strong hands around my face, kissing me softly on the lips.

His mouth was pillowy and strong and his lips felt like sparks of static on mine. As he pulled away, I felt his fingers place what felt like a tiny piece of paper in my hand. Before I could respond, or catch my breath, he slid into the driver's seat of his dark sedan and drove away.

I watched his taillights until they became tiny red eyes in the distance before I remembered the paper. Opening my hand, I found a small red heart, folded origami style, made from his gum wrapper. When I looked back to the road, his car was gone.

Chapter Six

ERIC

I slammed my fist on the wheel of the car in frustration as I pulled out of the hotel parking lot. Goddamn it, I wanted her so bad. What the hell was I thinking anyway? I wasn't going to be that guy anymore. I especially wasn't going to make her regret even seeing me again and that's all that would happen if we ended up at one of our hotel rooms for the night. I was a better person now and I swore I'd never be that player again.

Of course, I never would have expected Charlie Hanson to show up in Hydrangea Falls. She hated this place more than I did. My advantage was that my past wasn't living here anymore, but hers was. And Davy was a past that anyone would love to forget.

Davy was an asshole. An absolute grade-A, grandma-robbing, cheating, alcoholic, always the perpetual teenager, motherfucker. And I hated him. Not just for how he treated Charlie back then, but for general reasons. Most of which was that I saw a little bit of myself in Davy and that made me sick. I never robbed my grandmother, but I'll admit, I caused my own trouble.

While Charlie was living her worst life with that scum of the earth, I was making my own mark on the world; namely bedding any woman I could. I knew I was good-looking back then. A boy in his sexual prime and the looks that made attracting the opposite sex even easier. Hell, I'm still at the gym six days a week. Back then, I was the crown king of one-night stands. That was my youth rebelling against normalcy. Against wiser men. Against boredom.

Goddamn it, I was a whore, and the crazier the woman, the more I liked it. That was until I met Marta.

Per my usual routine, we met at a bar one night after I hustled a couple of co-workers in a pool tournament. She walked up to me and handed me a shot of something that tasted like heaven and burned like hell on the way down. Her signature move, the one that put her over the top that night, was the way she licked the remains of fiery liquid off my lips. I had her that night. And the night after that, and the night after that. I didn't think I would ever get enough of her curves, her soft skin, or her midnight-colored eyes. But, after a week, and again, per my normal pattern back then, I got bored with her. I hadn't been in a relationship since high school and back then, had zero desire for one.

I did what came naturally at the time. I avoided her, ignored her, and refused to return any of her calls. Marta didn't take my dodging well, to say the least. Understandably, she was upset;

after all, I was being a dick. But, her anger quickly became an obsession that turned into a threat to my life; something *I* couldn't ignore.

I grew up after Marta and getting older changes your perspective, especially when it comes to your choice of a woman. No longer willing to be the playboy of my past, I now want someone who's smart, kind and has lived their own life. I've been dating at home and I have just about given up on finding the woman I'm looking for—

Until tonight.

I think I just drove away from the woman I am meant to be with.

Chapter Seven

CHARLIE

Shutting off the ignition of my car, I sat in the lot of my hotel for a long moment. I watched an older man with a tattered brown suitcase walk into the foyer of the hotel for a late check-in as I ran the entire night through my head. I wondered if I had given Eric the wrong signals earlier. It was so nice to run into him after so long, maybe I was too eager to be friendly.

Scoffing aloud, I turned to see if anyone heard me chuckling alone in my car because being eagerly friendly didn't sound like me at all. It was a hysterical joke that few would find as funny as I did.

I watched another car pull into the parking lot as I theorized over the reasons for his quick departure. Showing up in the Falls was difficult enough for me, even before my parents died, now I was getting the itchy feeling that I couldn't put this town in my rearview mirror fast enough. I only had two days left here; I could make it work. Besides, I still haven't had the chance to see Josie yet. No one could be anything but happy in her presence and spending time with her would make me forget all about the weirdness with Eric. Still frustrated, I slid out of the car and trudged to the doors of the building when my phone rang.

Struggling to pull it from my tiny purse, my voice was angry when I finally answered.

"Hello?" I barked.

There was a short pause.

"Uhm, yes, is this Charlotte Hanson?" a meek woman asked.

"Yes, this is Charlie. What can I do for you?" I softened my tone as I spoke, realizing how harsh I must have sounded.

"Ms. Hanson, this is Carla White, I'm a nurse here at St. Vincent Hospital. Are you the niece of Nettie Carter?" Carla asked, her voice sounding distant like she was on the brink of being out of cell service range.

My gut started to send the all too familiar signals of doom to my brain. Like flipping a switch, I became Special Agent Hanson.

"Yes, Nettie is my aunt. What's the matter?" I demanded firmly.

Carla cleared her throat, "Ms. Hanson, we need to you come to St. Vincent's immediately...there has been an accident. Your aunt is in the emergency room with injuries sustained in a fire—"

"A what!?" I interrupted. "Where? Where was the fire? Is my aunt alright? What about Josie? Where is her daughter?"

I tried to remain calm, but there were important questions that needed answers. I spun on the ball of my foot, charging back to my car.

"Ma'am...I don't know where her daughter is," the nurse's voice broke like she might cry. "We are asking you to come to St. Vincent's—"

I was already in the vehicle and turning onto the freeway onramp, "I'm on my way."

Chapter Eight

DARKNESS

The phone's receiver slid from my hand. Someone would get to the old woman in time, surely. I gave them ample opportunity to pull her from the building. I couldn't be blamed for what might happen, because I had no idea that someone, or even two someones, would be in that place at this time of night. Why were they there? I thought I had chosen my target well.

I can't change it. It's not my problem.

They will find the old woman.

My Dearest would be on their way and I had a message to deliver. Hopefully, this time, they're paying attention. Hopefully this time, they listen.

After all these years, I'm tired of being ignored.

CHAPTER NINE

ERIC

Deciding that I wouldn't go back to my hotel room, I roared past it, heading into Hydrangea Falls. It was well after midnight, but I could use the quiet drive in the cool spring air. This wasn't something that was uncommon for me. I often drove around the desert surrounding Vegas for hours after a shift if I just couldn't shut my brain down for the night. Reaching under my seat, I grabbed my GPS-equipped scanner and flipped the switch on. For some reason, I found the buzzes, clicks, and static voices calming.

I came upon the main street square, driving slowly around the courthouse at its center. It looked like a small, European castle with its whitewashed stone and turrets. Dim light filtered from the windows and spilled onto the well-kept lawn. With each left turn, I gazed at the rows of shuttered buildings lining the opposite side of the street that had once held a variety of mom-and-pop businesses and were now lost to time. A few were seeing a resurgence of life, but I wondered how long it would be until they were also closed.

Flashes of my past perforated my mind as I took another pass around the square. I thought of cruising in my old Ford truck with its rusted edges on warm summer nights with a gang of friends riding in the bed. We pulled into parking spots to drink beer and laugh until the local cop told us to leave around midnight. I saw the ghosts of spring carnivals and fall festivals with their distinct and pungent scent of popcorn, cotton candy, and caramel apples filling my nostrils...

The scanner popped and crackled to life.

"All units, all units...name of survivor...Carter, Annette... seventy-nine-year-old female...resides in Hydrangea Falls. Medics en route to St. Vincents...possible broken leg, smoke inhalation..."

Stomping on my brakes in the middle of the deserted street, the car screeched to a halt. Annette Carter?! The scanner crackled again.

"Be advised, we have Timberview Baptist Church contact Henry Simmons en route. He's been advised it's a total loss..."

"Holy shit," I said aloud as I romped on the gas, heading in the direction of St. Vincent's.

CHAPTER TEN

CHARLIE

My car came to a rigid stop in the first parking spot I could find. The red lights of the EMERGENCY sign overhead created an eerie glow on the sidewalk as I barreled through the automated doors. After locating the nurse's desk, I stood patiently for my turn before finding out my aunt had just arrived and was being worked on by personnel.

"I would like to speak to the paramedics who brought her in," I requested with authority.

"Ma'am, the medics are very busy...they don't have time to talk to family—" a short red-headed nurse drawled before noticing my FBI credentials being held in her face.

I hated myself for pulling the fed card, but if it got me the information I wanted, I'd play the game for now. The stubby nurse's eyes widened as she stared at the badge.

"Ma'am...you can go through that door right there," she said, reaching over and pushing a button under the desk.

On the far left of the nurse's triage station was a set of electronic double doors leading to the emergency room patient area. I moved through the narrow white hallways until I came to another round desk that teamed with medical personnel. At the far end of the station, I saw two paramedics, one male, and one female, writing on clipboards and speaking with a uniformed Portland Police officer. I knew I found who I was looking for.

"Excuse me?" I said. "Are you the medics that brought in Nettie Carter?"

The male, a blonde-haired, blue-eyed young man no older than twenty-five nodded, "If you mean Annette Carter, then yes. What can we do for you?"

"I'm looking for what happened tonight...I was told there was a fire?" I began.

The police officer broke in, "Are you next of kin?"

I nodded, "Yes, My name is Charlotte Hanson, I'm her niece. Someone called."

The officer flipped pages on a tiny notepad as if confirming the information before he spoke again.

"I have she has a daughter...a Josie Carter?" he asked.

I nodded, "Yes. If she wasn't with her mother, she can be found at her apartment in Newburg."

He scribbled notes on his pad, "Would you happen to have her number? We need to contact her to let her know about her mother."

"No...I'm advising you not to do that. I will pick her up and bring her here. She'll need to be with family," I countered.

I saw the officer becoming impatient with me, as his narrow jaw flexed, "Ma'am...we are adept at making notifications to family members. Along with the open and ongoing investigation, her next of kin will need to be notified. That *is* our job, please let us do it."

He turned to walk away. I knew what he was saying because I had been in his shoes. I wouldn't be able to count how many times I had run-ins with extended families under similar circumstances; everyone jumping the line to be given any information first. I knew the man was just doing his job, but I was over the niceties and I was going to get some damn answers.

"Excuse me," I demanded firmly, pulling my federal ID out of my purse again, showed it to him, and then read his nameplate over his pocket: *Duran*. "Officer Duran, consider notification made. Mrs. Carter's daughter is special needs and is very close to her mother. I would prefer that a uniformed police officer not scare her this late at night. Now, as you can see I am fully educated and well-versed in investigative procedures and I have questions. Would you like to answer them or should I call your CO?"

The man seemed to turn green at my badge, but I thought I saw the female paramedic cut a satisfied grin in my direction. She reached over, shaking my hand.

"Hi...I'm Deana. We were called to the Timberview Baptist Church around ten on reports of a fire. When we arrived, firefighters were already pulling your aunt out of the building. My partner and I immediately began working on her and brought her here in our bus," she explained.

"A fire in the church?" I looked at the officer. "What started it?"

Duran shook his head, "We don't know yet. A fire investigator will be out at first light to go through the rubble."

"Rubble? As in—" I prodded.

"As in, *to* the ground, ma'am," the officer shook his head. "I'm sorry ma'am, that's all I know."

He handed me a card.

"Please, if you have questions...don't hesitate to call the precinct. I believe your aunt is in room two for now...but I overheard something about surgery. I'll find a nurse for you," he closed his notebook and left.

I thanked Deana and her partner before they also made their way to leave. After a few minutes, a young nurse came out to tell me that my aunt wouldn't be able to have visitors and that she was being taken into surgery for the broken leg. After giving the nurse my cell phone number, I found my way back out into the ER waiting room. As I rounded the corner of the locked door of the unit, and around the triage station, I heard a familiar voice calling my name. I turned to see the broad shoulders of Eric Tilset walking in my direction.

Chapter Eleven

ERIC

"What are you doing here?" Charlie asked me, her normally sparkling woody eyes now dark and sunken.

I didn't know what to do. I wanted to pull her into me and tell her it would all be fine, even when I knew the opposite was probably true. I had been on the job long enough to know that.

"I heard on the scanner. Charlie, I'm so sorry. How is she?" I asked gently.

Charlie shook her head, "I don't know. They won't let me see her...they're taking her into surgery now to try and repair her leg." She sighed and continued, "I'm going out to the church now. I've got to see what happened."

"Why don't I drive?" I offered. I didn't want her out there alone and she was much too exhausted to drive. Her eyes became round and almost thankful for my offer.

"I can't ask you to do that," she replied.

"I didn't hear you ask," I smiled softly at her.

On the way, we made a stop at her hotel room so she could change out of her suit and heels. Five minutes after parking my car, Charlie was walking back out of the automated hotel doors dressed in jeans, boots, and a dark hoodie with *Annapolis Naval Academy* emblazoned on the front. I cocked an eyebrow at her when she shut the door to the sedan.

"Nice sweatshirt," I commented dryly. "Didn't know you were in the Navy too."

She looked down as if she didn't realize what she had grabbed to put on.

"Oh. No, not me...ex-boyfriend. He kept the condo...I got the sweatshirt," she chuckled.

I laughed, "Who got the better deal?"

"Definitely me," Charlie smiled tiredly.

I recognized the look of exhaustion on her face. It wasn't just being weary at the end of a long day; it was the kind of distressed, straining, annoying fatigue that anyone in our line of work has experienced. Part of your body wants to give up, but there's a switch that just refuses to shut down. It keeps your mind awake, your heart racing, and your muscles ready for the next hit. This situation was only made worse by the fact that it was Nettie who was hurt and not a stranger.

After weaving our way through the gentle curves of the wooded areas that blanketed Hydrangea Falls, we turned down the narrow county road of Timberview. We made it only half a mile when flashes of lights and the familiar smell of water and burned wood, metal, and plastic assaulted our nostrils. I pulled the sedan off to one side, out of the way of the firefighters rolling hoses and repacking the trucks.

We sloshed through thick mud, making our way around two engines that blocked our view before a young man stopped us.

"I'm sorry...you can't be here," he held up his hands.

Rookies are fun.

"Bobby around?" I asked and I swear the kid turned white.

"Chief Miller, you mean?" the probie stuttered. His voice cracked a little and reminded me of my own pre-pubescence.

"Yeah, he available?" I prodded again.

The kid's eyes narrowed on me, "No, he's not. Can I help you?"

I almost laughed out loud and I admired the kid's spirit, probably because I'd been just like him at one time. I didn't want to give the kid too much shit, but Bobby Miller and I went way back. But I also didn't want to waste too much time since Nettie probably didn't have much of it left.

"Look, kid," I put on my friendliest, and firmest, grin, "That's Bob's Tahoe...so, I know he's around. Not to mention there was a woman pulled out of this and put on a bus two hours ago. Now, get on your radio and tell him to get his fat ass over here."

That last part was just for fun since while I was talking to the kid, a large man walked up behind the young probie and stood. The young man's face turned another shade of white, staring at me trying to determine if I was serious, or not, and if he should do exactly what I said, or not. The round, mustached, face of Bob Miller widened into a giant smile.

"Belay that order, Michaels," his voice bellowed, making the kid jump out of his skin. "The hell are you doing all the way out here, Probie?"

The kid opened his mouth to speak before I cut him off. I knew Bob was referring to me.

"It's the damnedest thing...my scanners' broken. Won't shut off," I replied.

Bob chortled loudly then cut his eyes at the kid. "You got somewhere to be?"

Micheals startled at Bob's voice, "Uh...yes sir!"

He scuttled off.

Bobby Miller was a barrel of a man who stood well over six foot, five inches tall. He had a Wilford Brimley mustache and cropped sandy brown hair. His voice was like scraping metal over gravel and he had a stare that would shake a giant. A person knew they were in the presence of a great behemoth when they met him, but few knew *how* great. He had been my trainer in fire school and my mentor. And he was the only one who could talk any sense to me back then. There was no one else on the planet like him. I still idolized the man.

Bob reached out his giant hand and I shook it.

"Sir? Still got your bluff in on the new ones, huh?" I ribbed.

"Well, they're not all little shits like you," Bobby's laughter was large and filled the space around him. He allowed it to die off before continuing. "Seriously, what brings you out here?"

I pointed to Charlie, "This is Charlie Hanson, Bob. Your guys pulled her aunt out of here earlier."

The pair shook hands.

"I'm sorry about your aunt, ma'am," he said sincerely.

Charlie nodded, "Can you determine what started the fire?"

"Well," Bob gave a fleeting glance at me. I knew what he was about to say and I also knew it wouldn't do any good.

"We really need to wait until the Marshal gets on the scene," he explained.

I could have mouthed the words as he said them. It was one of the things I learned from him all those years ago: Don't give too much away to the family because if you're wrong or miss-peak, they will never forget it and it will be the only thing they remember. But I also knew this time it was different. Charlie wasn't just some family member who didn't have a clue about how an investigation works. She was trained and this was well within her wheelhouse. I knew all of this, but Bob didn't.

"Hey, Bob," I interrupted. "She's a Fed. She knows. What can you tell us off the record?"

He nodded, lifting the crime scene tape so we could pass. We walked along either side of the larger-than-life man and closer to the collapse zone.

"Not a lot yet. Accelerant was used...you can see that from the obvious burn patterns. We'll know in a couple of days what kind," Bob explained.

"So, arson?" Charlie asked.

He nodded, "Most likely. And a total loss...not even a pew left. This was a hot fire...your aunt is lucky we got the call when we did."

"What do you mean?" I asked.

"First due rolled out at nine-thirty. When they arrived, the building was still smoking...most of the accelerant hadn't caught yet," Bob replied.

"So, when did it become fully involved?" I asked.

"Fully involved?" Charlie arched a brow.

"When the fire engulfs the whole building," I explained then nodded at the Chief to continue.

"Just after we extricated. Whole damn room went up," Bob continued to walk around the outside of the zone at a safe distance.

We moved to survey the destruction as we wove around teams of firefighters and hoses. We finally made it around to the back of what was left of the large church where a back door formerly stood. I say formally because there was nearly nothing left. Cinderblock and wood were turned to hot ash in front of us and the heat that emanated from the now non-existent edifice was still sweltering. Charlie took a step back to move away from it and nearly tripped herself as her foot rolled over something.

"What's that?" she said, bending down to pick it up. The glass bottle was amber in color and missing its lid. Before I could stop her, she lifted it to her nose to smell the contents.

I watched as her eyes rolled to the back of her head and I scrambled to catch her.

Chapter Twelve

CHARLIE

My head swam and the flashing lights of the fire and police vehicles were dizzying. I felt like I was floating on air before I realized Eric was carrying me. I wriggled to get out of his arms.

"Put...me down..." I said, my head lolling side to side.

He rolled his eyes, "Jesus...wait a second. Let me get you to the car."

My head snapped straight and our eyes met for a split second before I fainted. A few moments later, I was drawing a deep breath, and speaking mid-sentence.

"I said put me down—"

I looked around to find Eric checking my pulse as I sat in the passenger side of his rented sedan. His green eyes looked through their long lashes at me, then back to his wristwatch.

"What've you eaten tonight?" he asked, not taking his eyes off his watch.

"What?" I snapped.

"You know...food? When's the last time you ate?" he put my wrist down on my lap but remained squatted next to me, staring.

I laid my head back, "I don't know...I'm fine."

"Charlie—" his voice demanded with concern.

"I went for a drive today. Grabbed a burger through a dri-ve-through," I barked.

Eric waited for the rest of the story but I only eyed him.

"That's it?" he asked incredulously.

"Just...don't. Okay? I'm fine...I don't need you hovering," I barked again. "I get less than that some days...I'm *fine*."

I barely knew him and I certainly didn't want him brooding over me like a mother hen. Jesus, who did this guy think he was?

Eric drew his lips in tight, "Yeah, you keep saying that."

I heard Bobby's graveled voice reverberating behind him, "Tilset, how's she doing?"

I noticed him walking toward us with a paramedic.

Eric sighed, rolling his eyes, "She's...*fine*...Bob. Needs to eat...I'm gonna take her back into town."

He abandoned his position next to me to shake the chief's hand.

"Sounds good, son. Look, I'll call you when we hear back about this place...keep me updated on Nettie, will ya?" Bobby asked.

"Sure thing," Eric promised, nodding. He walked around the car and slid into the driver's seat. As the engine roared to life, he turned to me, still feeling pale next to him.

"Food first...then we go back to the hospital. Agreed?"

I nodded. What choice did I have, really?

CHAPTER THIRTEEN

ERIC

I should have told her what happened; I know. But, she had enough on her plate at the moment and I didn't want to add to any suspicions just yet. I also didn't know what was in that bottle that she stuck her nose into, but when she woke up, she didn't mention it, so neither did I. I gave it over to Bobby to tag as evidence for the Fire Marshal. Besides, food would do her some good right now.

In a small town like Hydrangea Falls, nothing stays open after ten. But, just a few miles up the road in towns like Beaverton, there was always someplace open twenty-four hours a day. Jersey Diner was one of those places that served breakfast all day with a side of coffee that could hold a spoon upright. I was sure Charlie hadn't been here since she was a teenager looking for someplace to hang out with friends on a late Saturday night. She was amused that nothing had changed, even the smell of greasy diner food. It was then I heard her stomach growling.

She was finishing her second cup of coffee when our very thin, clearly overworked waitress sat plates of food in front of us. The smell of freshly cooked bacon, eggs, hash browns, and buttered toast made her eyes roll with pleasure. Charlie realized then that maybe, just *maybe* she wasn't fine like she thought. She loaded scrambled eggs and hashbrowns on her fork and took a giant bite.

"I forgot about how good this place was," she chewed.

Cutting into a sausage link, I mused, "I know. Brings back memories."

"Oh yeah? You too?" Charlie bit a slice of bacon in half.

"Mhmm," I nodded with a mouth full of food. "Do you remember Dylan Groff? He and I used to come in here every weekend...we thought it was cool to bring dates here for coffee after the movies."

"Dates, huh?" Charlie mused. "I don't remember you dating anyone in our class."

Shaking my head, I chuckled, "I didn't...at least not while we were in school."

"How'd you end up in Vegas, anyway?" she asked. She watched me cut into my egg and take a bite.

"After graduation, I became a paramedic. Then I went to the firefighter academy in Portland. Bobby was an instructor. I met a girl...followed her to Vegas...the rest is history," I answered casually.

"Whoa! The rest is history? What does that mean?" Charlie chuckled.

"Just what it sounds like...history. The past...not worth talking about," I took another bite of food. My words told her it was a break-up, but apparently, my tone told her just how bad it was.

"I'm sorry," her voice was filled with gentle kindness. It was unnecessary, but I did appreciate the emotion behind it.

Charlie finished her meal and sipped a fresh cup of coffee. I watched her and could almost see her mind racing with all the things she needed to do. She watched me fold my tea bag much like I had done earlier in the night with the gum wrapper. Before she knew it, she saw the tiny heart appear as if it were magic. When I was finished, I looked across the table at her.

"Feel better?" I asked.

Charlie nodded.

"Good," I continued. "We'll head back to the hospital to check on Nettie. As soon as it's daylight, we can go see Josie."

Charlie stared at me for a moment.

"Look," she returned her cup to the table. "I appreciate every-thing...but, I'm a big girl. I can take care of myself."

My eyes narrowed on her, "Why are you so goddamn stub-born?"

She glared daggers at me and I could almost hear her thoughts. Who the hell did I think I was? She didn't ask for me to show up at the hospital and she certainly didn't ask me to escort her to the scene of the fire. She could take care of her own business and didn't need an old classmate's help. She pulled a fifty-dollar bill from her pocket and threw it on the table.

"Thanks for the ride out to the church...I think I'll take a cab from here," she slid across the booth and walked out of the door.

Damn it.

I sat motionless for a long moment, watching her pull out her cell phone to make a call. As she turned her back to me to talk into the receiver, my heart pulled for her. Until I saw her tonight, I never imagined I would feel the immediate connection with someone that I did with her. I didn't want to screw it up. I spent most of my adult life hopping from one one-night stand to another. I had my reasons; sometimes it was better not to get too emotionally involved. But, when I saw Charlie, even after all these years, I couldn't help myself; my world turned upside down.

But now wasn't the right time. She didn't need someone to ask her on a date. Hell, she didn't think she needed anyone at all. Ever. But, I saw that church and experience told me that Nettie wasn't out of the woods yet. I would be there for Charlie.

As I took the last sip of my tea, I glanced out the window and saw a look of despair wash over her. I could tell she was trying to hold herself together but was failing miserably. Her tear-filled eyes shot in my direction as I rushed out of the diner's glass doors.

"What is it?" I ordered. I heard the beep on her phone as the call disconnected.

"Aunt Nettie. Eric...we have to go. Now."

Chapter Fourteen

CHARLIE

I hit the buzzer twice on the locked doors of the intensive care unit. The nurse on the phone told me to come immediately and even though visiting hours were several hours away, they would make an exception in my aunt's case.

"Yes?" a woman's voice crackled over the speaker.

"Charlie Hanson here to see Nettie Carter...someone called," my voice shook.

The speaker crackled again, "Yes, ma'am. I'll buzz you in."

I looked up at Eric and his kind eyes fell over me. Despite what I had just said to him in the diner, it was comforting that he was there with me. I never seemed to need anyone in life except my partner, Jack. But, right now, I needed Eric.

"I'll wait here," he said softly.

My heart raced. I knew by the sound of the voice over the phone that my aunt's condition was dire. And even though throughout my career I had been involved in high-speed car chases, shoot-outs, and a hostage situation or two, *this* moment terrified me. I could call it nerves, flashbacks, or even a trauma response, but I did not want to walk through those doors alone.

The door buzzed and the lock released.

Grabbing Eric's large hand, I shook my head, "No. I...really don't want to be alone."

Eric nodded, lacing his fingers with mine.

The unit itself was wider than it was long. We took notice that fourteen glass rooms surrounded a large, round nurse's station. The lights were dim and other than the occasional beep of a monitor, it was quiet. As we approached the edge of the desk, an older woman with mousy-gray hair rose from her chair.

"Hello...I'm Kathy, Annette's nurse. You must be Charlie," she introduced herself in hushed tones.

I nodded, "This is...Eric. Can you explain what's going on?"

Kathy walked around the edge of the desk and motioned for us to follow her. As we rounded the curve of the opposite side, Kathy pointed into room nine. I glanced in but noticed the curtains were pulled all around the bed.

"We can talk here before you see her," Kathy explained. "Your aunt suffered a crushed tibia and fibula in the left leg...that's something that could be fixed but—"

"But?" I prodded impatiently.

"But...Mrs. Carter's lungs are severely damaged due to the smoke and there's brain swelling. They were able to release some of the pressure, but we just don't know if it was enough. The prognosis isn't good. I am sorry," the nurse clarified. "I understand she has a daughter?"

My entire body was shaking. Eric could feel it and his grasp on my hand tightened. I closed my eyes to concentrate on the words the kind nurse was speaking, but their understanding was beyond me.

"Mrs. Hanson?" reaching out, Kathy touched my arm.

"Ms. Hanson...yes, she has a daughter Jos-ie," my voice broke and I took a deep breath. "I...uhhh...I was waiting for daylight to tell her. She...uh...she—"

Kathy looked at Eric.

"She has Down's Syndrome and has an apartment in New-burg. We were heading there when you called," he replied softly.

The nurse nodded, "I understand. If you can get her here as soon as possible, it would be for the best. If there is any more family that needs to be called, do that also."

Eric's face fell. He knew Josie and I were the only ones left; there was no more family to call.

"We'll take care of it...can she see her?" he asked.

"Of course...stay as long as you need...I'll go get another chair," she turned on her heel and left.

Chapter Fifteen

ERIC

Sunrise came soon enough into the critical care unit of St. Vincents. I sat with Charlie for the rest of the night while she held her dying aunt's hand. My heart ached for her. What a completely shitty way to come back home. It couldn't get any worse, right?

Wrong.

We just made our way down the elevator and into the large entrance of the hospital only to find Charlie's ex-husband, Davy Wyatt arguing with an older volunteer at the information desk.

"I want to see my aunt now!" he ground his teeth at the woman.

"Sir...you aren't on the visitor's list. I cannot give you any information on Ms. Carter," the graying woman replied.

Charlie sighed under her breath, "Mother. Fucker."

Before I could offer to handle it, she turned and marched toward the desk. I followed her lead. Which, to my credit, was the smart thing to do because I wanted to throw him out of that hospital on his bony ass. Davy Wyatt was a loser in high school and nothing had changed.

"Davy, you need to leave," Charlie ordered.

Davy's head whipped around as if he were ready for a fight. His eyes widened when he saw her and a look of shock spread across his face.

I'm not going to lie, it was satisfying to watch.

"Charlie. Wh...what," he stammered. "How did you get here so fast?"

"When did you make bail?" Charlie demanded.

Davy leaned on the desk as the woman behind the counter watched their exchange while slowly picking up the phone receiver. I knew what she was probably thinking; if things got out of hand, she wanted to have security there immediately. What she didn't know was that I wasn't going to let it get that far.

"Not that it's any of your business, but I got out this morning," Davy growled. "I heard about Nettie...I was worried."

"Bullshit," Charlie replied flatly.

"I don't have to explain myself to you. I ain't worried about some cop from another state," his unshaven lip curled in a snarl.

Charlie smiled at him. It wasn't one of pleasure or even kindness. It was cold. It was calculated. It was a damn turn-on. I never saw where it came from, because it was a slick movement, but before I knew it, she placed her badge on the counter in front of them. That dangerous smile never moved from her lips. She spoke in a low tone that only the three of us and the attendant could hear.

"Jesus, Davy, are we really going to do this?" she said calmly.

He stared at the badge and I swear the veins in his balding head were beating faster.

"I don't know what you think you're doing here, but from the look of the flop sweat, you're up to no good." Charlie picked up her credentials and slid them back into a pocket of her jeans, "I suggest you make the smart choice, for once in your miserable life, and walk out that door."

She pointed toward the bank of glass for effect.

Davy swallowed hard, staring at her for a long moment. He moved away from Charlie slowly before turning his back to us.

"Oh, and Davy?" she called after him. He turned back around to face her.

"If I catch you here again, trying to get near *my* aunt...I'll make a call to the judge and get your bail revoked."

He never responded except to turn around and run out of the automatic doors. I had never seen someone tuck their tail quicker than he did. She put enough scare into him that I was sure he wouldn't show his face again. I also realized something else at that moment, something I hope I get the chance to tell her.

I think I just fell in love.

Chapter Sixteen

CHARLIE

I couldn't roll my eyes hard enough. What a goddamn mess.

Of all days and places to run into my piece of shit ex-husband, it just had to be in that hospital. I knew Davy Wyatt well enough to know what he was doing there and it didn't have anything to do with concern for my aunt. My first guess? Drugs. Or Money.

As a matter of fact, Nettie and Davy had a mutual hatred of each other. While my parents were always okay to tow the *'As long as she's happy, it's fine with us'* line when it came to my relationship with Davy, Aunt Nettie was always a straight shooter. She hated him and made no bones about it. And when I needed a little extra help when I filed for my divorce from the asshole, Nettie was there; no questions asked. There was no doubt in my mind that Davy was only there to steal or snort whatever he could that wasn't nailed down.

I took a deep breath as we watched him haul ass out of the hospital. Looking over at Eric, I sighed, "Let's go pick up Josie."

Josie.

My funny, beautiful, expressive, much younger cousin, Josie. Aunt Nettie always wanted to have children, but couldn't ever get pregnant. She and her husband, my Uncle Bill, had given up and taken on the role of the spoilers of children in our family. It was always a fun time at Nettie and Bill's. They lived in Hydrangea Falls in a large Victorian on a neatly kept corner lot four blocks off the center of town. They hosted almost all of our family holiday festivities and a yearly neighborhood Halloween party.

It was at one of these parties that Aunt Nettie fell ill, nearly fainting into the tub of apples for the apple bob. I was a young teen then, but even I knew that there was something seriously wrong with her. A week later, they proudly announced that they would be expecting a new baby in early summer. I remember my mom talking with Nettie about all of her doctor's appointments and how risky her pregnancy was, especially for someone *her age*. But neither Nettie nor Bill cared; they were just overjoyed that they were finally going to be parents.

Josie Angelica Carter was born on June 21, 1987, and weighed in at six pounds, twelve ounces. She had ten fingers and ten toes and a head full of white-blonde hair that nearly overtook her tiny, perfectly round head. She was also born with what the doctors called Trisomy twenty-one but what is commonly referred to as Down's syndrome. She was a perfect baby.

Even though I was thirteen years older, I grew up close to Josie. She was my buddy and best friend since the day she was born. I loved her more than anyone, even though I had to admit

I'd been a terrible friend to her over the past decade. I was realizing that now and I felt guilty.

Eric pulled in front of her row apartment and shut off the engine. I stared at the paned window with its pretty lace curtains and freshly painted window box planter. I hadn't laid eyes on Josie in more than ten years; not since my parent's funerals. I did write, though, when I could. I sent Easter cards and Halloween cards and made sure she got flowers on her birthday. Still, I felt guilty for not taking the time to drive a little over two damn hours to see her on the holidays.

Shit.

"Charlie, we can't wait for long. She needs to see her mother," Eric prodded me.

I sighed, "I know."

We barely stepped out of the car when the front door opened and Josie's long blonde hair was glistening in the morning sun. She let out a shriek of joy when she saw me.

"Charlie!" she squealed as she ran toward me. "You...yo...You should have called."

She stutters a bit; I had forgotten that. She threw her arms around me, resting her head on my chest as she was about a foot and a half shorter than me. I hugged her back tightly. I had no idea how I was going to tell her about her mother.

"I know, Josie. I'm sorry we came by without calling. Can we go inside and talk?" I asked.

She looked around me at Eric, "Wh...Wh...Who's that?"

"You remember Eric Tilset, don't you? He lived on the other side of the creek from me when we were younger," I smiled.

"Yes! I d...d...do!" her grin filled her face. "Yo...yo...you showed me how to catch craw...crawdads."

Josie's eyes glistened with recognition and they squinted a little when she formed her words. I suddenly became acutely aware of the small mannerisms in Josie that reminded me of her mother. The tiny tilt of her head toward Eric showed interest in his upcoming reply. The minuscule wrinkles around her eyes when she smiled and the soft stroke of her fingers on my wrist as she held onto me. Every one of these traits is identical to her mother.

Eric beamed at her, "Yes, I did. You've got a great memory...I forgot about that."

Josie's smile was still angelic and bright. I hated myself that I would be the one to take it away today. It was so damn unfair that what should be a happy reunion between cousins would be marred by trauma and sadness.

And death.

I had to redirect my thoughts. I couldn't bear to think about what my instinct was screaming at me. It was too much right now to dwell on and too much for her to know.

"Jos...let's go inside and talk."

Chapter Seventeen
CHARLIE

Josie was still crying as Eric drove us back to St. Vincent's. I sat in the back with her and held her close to me. The late spring sun warmed us as I stroked her soft hair in my hands. I worried about what would become of her if Nettie died.

When. Not if.

The pit in my stomach that had been softly gnawing at me had now consumed all of my insides. I knew what that feeling meant. I learned to trust it and use it often. It only came when something was about to go sideways.

Nettie would have said it's my guardian angel speaking to me with a warning. Aunt Nettie holds on to her religious beliefs. My good friend from college, Gabrielle, would say that I'm tuned in to the natural vibrations of the life force that surrounds every being. She's a new-age hippie who believes in crystals and candle magic. But I'm logical and I have experiences that my subconscious mind forms into recognizable patterns. My brain then alerts my body to those patterns.

You know, science.

My aunt would die. My mind knew it and my heart and body were now catching up to that fact. Eric knew it also, but he was too kind to throw it in my face. He probably understood her injuries better than I did but didn't want me to lose hope. He was trying to be someone I could lean on, and at the moment, I appreciated his concern.

I had to be strong for Josie. She was going to lose her mother.

"Shhh...I know, Jos. Eric will get us there as fast as possible," I locked eyes with him in the rearview mirror. He read between the lines and I felt the sedan lurch, racing faster toward the hospital.

It was a good thing he did because as Josie held her mother's hand and stroked her wrinkled cheek, the monitor that measured each heartbeat flatlined. Nurses raced into the room, putting themselves between the three of us and Nettie's bed. I struggled with a wailing Josie as she fought to get back to her mother. My body shook with fear and exhaustion and sadness.

Once in the hallway, my cousin buried her head into my chest and sobbed, "Ma-ma!"

I looked into Eric's face, but instead of empathy, I saw anger. It took me back for a moment. But as sudden as it was, his expression melted quickly into grief. He moved forward, enveloping the pair of us in warmth and comfort.

In my career, I have dealt with hundreds of grieving families. And while almost all of them followed the five steps of grief, no two were exactly alike. As I stood in Eric's embrace, I wondered for a fleeting moment how mine would be different from theirs.

I had no time for denial. This was actually happening and there was nothing I could do to stop it.

Acceptance.

Little did I know that while I might have skipped a step, or two, I would come back to those in due time. Eric's deep voice interrupted my thoughts.

"Charlie," he whispered in my ear.

I looked up to find one of the nurses standing in the doorway of Nettie's room. The moment we locked eyes, her head shook.

Nettie was gone.

Giant tears welled in my eyes, but I fought them back before Josie could see me cry. Eric released us and I held my cousin out away from my body so I could look her in the eyes.

"Jos...Nettie's gone. I'm so sorry, sweetheart."

Chapter Eighteen

ERIC

"Is she with Jesus now?"

The tiny, innocent question dug into my heart. *Goddamn it.*

"Yeah, Jos, she is," Charlie pulled Josie against her again, allowing her to cry a little longer.

"I want to see her. Wi...wi...will they let me see her?" she asked through softening sobs.

I laid my hand on her back, "I'm sure they will...let me go in first and make sure it's okay."

I looked at Charlie for approval and she nodded. I really hoped I wasn't overstepping, but I didn't know what else to do. I'm the helper. The one that takes care of business and I couldn't fix anything this time. After poking my head back into the wide room and asking if it was alright if we returned, I nodded to the pair and followed them back inside.

After removing wires and intravenous lines, the staff did a quick, but efficient tidy of Nettie's gown and bed sheets. Aside from the head bandage and bruising on her face, she looked as though she could be sleeping. Josie walked over, picking up her mother's hand.

"M...mm...Mama," she whispered and leaned down, kissing the woman on the cheek. "I hope you and...da...d... Daddy have a nice visit."

Anger boiled inside me. Whoever set that fire was going to pay. I would make sure of it. If not for Nettie, for Josie and Charlie. The senseless act wouldn't go unpunished, I would see to it. The sadness in Josie's eyes ripped me to pieces.

We stayed for a while longer, until Josie was ready to leave, before making our way back downstairs. I waited with her while Charlie spoke with the desk attendant about releasing Nettie's body to the funeral home. Once she was finished we quietly piled back into my car and sat in silence. I think we were all numb with shock. I felt terrible that I couldn't offer either of them any words of comfort. I started the engine, backing out of the parking spot when Charlie's door unexpectedly flew open, nearly denting the vehicle next to us.

It took me a moment to catch a glimpse of what she was targeting. The second my eyes registered with my brain, I slammed the gear shift into park and threw open my door.

"Josie, stay here!" I ordered with a gentle command.

"Charlie!" I bellowed as I sprinted after her. But before I could reach her, she already caught her prey. Charlie wrapped her fist into Davy's dirty tee shirt and spun him in place, slamming him into a nearby truck.

"You son of a bitch! *You* had something to do with this, didn't you?" she screamed.

Davy's bloodshot eyes were wide with anger, "Crazy bitch! Get your hands off me!"

The scrawny man shoved her hard enough that she fell into a neighboring sport-utility vehicle; a white four-door type with a stick family on the back window.

As she lunged at him again, I jumped between them, throwing a right punch that landed squarely on his jaw. Davy fell back on his ass onto the pavement. He immediately tried to get up.

"Stay down!" I pointed at Davy's face.

"I can handle this!" Charlie shoved me out of the way. "I don't need *you* to save the day!"

"I'm not rescuing you," I spun her around to face me all the while keeping an eye on the little weasel in my peripheral. He was trying to get up again. "I told you to stay down."

I turned back to Charlie, "Don't lose your career over this asshole."

"I want to know why he's still hanging around. My aunt just died and I want to know what he knows about it!"

She was fuming.

"Wait. Nettie's dead?" A smirk was growing across Davy's gaunt face.

Charlie stared at him with fury, "You think that's funny?"

"Just a good day, that's all. Ol' bitch can't keep me from helping my mom run her errands anymore," he laughed.

Charlie lunged, "You mean stealing drugs from your arthritic, wheel-chair bound mother, you piece of shit?"

I pointed at Davy again as I grabbed Charlie's arm, "I'm telling you one time, Wyatt...keep your mouth shut or I'll turn her loose."

I don't know if it was those words that triggered Charlie back into reality, or if she came to it on her own, but I felt her body stop fighting against me as her arm relaxed in my hold. I wasn't saving *her*, I was saving *him*. An act that went against every fiber of my being and that I regretted seconds later.

I lowered my voice, "Go back to the car. Josie needs you."

Charlie scowled and lunged at him once more for good measure before turning on the heel of her combat boot. I watched her walk back to the car before I turned to Davy pulling himself off the blacktop, a dirty grin still on his face.

"Hey! Tell the retard I said hi—"

I threw another right hook, but this time, my aim was better and I caught him in the nose. Blood sprayed wildly across the cars parked nearby and he fell to the ground again.

"I told you to keep your fucking mouth shut, dumbass!" I yelled. I looked down at him as pooled blood mixed with the tears falling from his chin. I leaned over close so he could hear me clearly. I didn't want him to misunderstand my next words.

"If you had anything to do with the fire that killed Nettie, I promise you'll not live to regret it," my eyes locked with his.

Davy's body shook as he nodded his head carefully. I was glad to see he understood that I meant every word.

CHAPTER NINETEEN

ERIC

After returning to the car, the ladies decided that we all could use a bite to eat; Josie especially. After running through her favorite fast-food joint, we drove her back to Nettie's home. Josie wanted to stay at her mother's house and decide what she would wear in the casket. The young woman looked comfortable and well-adjusted to the home and was very direct in telling us to leave.

"I'll be alright Ch...Ch...Charlie," Josie patted her cousin on the shoulder.

She shook her head, "I don't know Josie...I don't think you should stay here alone. I mean...what will you do for dinner? Or for clothes tomorrow?"

Josie seemed to take offense to her cousin's seeming ignorance, "I know how to c...c...cook! And I always keep cl...c...clothes at Mama's. I'm not an in...in...invalid."

Charlie looked hurt, but I knew she was only trying to help. She wasn't thinking clearly and for good reason. Neither one of us had slept in almost thirty hours. Risking Charlie thinking I was interfering or *saving* her, I interjected.

"Hey, Josie, why don't I get her out of here and back to the hotel? We'll let you get settled and come back in the morning," I turned to face Charlie. "I know there will be a lot of decisions tomorrow and you both could use some rest."

To my surprise, Charlie nodded and I followed her toward the door with Josie bringing up the rear.

"Okay, I'll see you tomorrow," she reached for the knob. "Jos, don't forget to lock the door."

Josie rolled her eyes like a defiant teenager.

"I'm sorry," Charlie reached out for her cousin's hand. "I love you, Jos."

"I...I...I love you too," her eyes twinkled as she shut the decorative door behind us.

Charlie waited until she heard both locks being engaged before wandering slowly down the painted concrete steps to the small picket gate. I heard her make a deep sigh and a ragged breath as she shut the car door. Turning the engine over, I glanced to see rivers flowing down her flawless cheeks. I watched her for a moment but she never took her eyes off the road.

It was as if she heard my question before I could ask it when she choked out, "Just drive."

So I drove. I had no destination or expectation in mind. I was finding out just what kind of woman Charlie Hanson was though. She was beautiful, strong, determined, and self-contained. She wanted no sympathy and quietly demanded respect from everyone she met. She was entirely self-made. She was everything I wanted and *needed* in my life and I wanted to be anything and everything for her. Right now she needed to grieve her aunt. Quietly, intimately. So I drove.

Before I realized where we were going, I absently turned down a dirty road that skirted an open field dotted with small clumps of tall trees. She wiped away the last remnants of tears from her chin and began actively looking out the window.

"Where are we?" She gasped, "Oh my God. This is your parents' place and that is—"

I blinked, "Uh...yeah. The creek."

I honestly didn't realize until that moment where we were. I shut off the engine and exited the vehicle with her. She looked around the pasture smiling.

"Wow. I haven't been here in..." her voice trailed off as we walked in the direction of the water.

"Years?" I asked.

Charlie closed her eyes, taking in a deep breath, "Yeah."

At the edge of the creek, I plucked a flat stone off the bank. Leaning back, I threw the rock sideways and watched it skim over the surface once, then twice before it plopped into the stream. I turned when I heard Charlie laughing.

"I still will never figure out how you skip stones on moving water," she sat hard in the grass.

I picked another pebble and threw it the same way again. This time, it jumped three times before landing several feet away. I walked back to where she sat, running her hands through the grass on either side of her.

"Lucky, I guess," I shrugged.

Charlie leaned back on her arms, tilting her head up toward the dappled sunlight peeking through the trees. She looked exhausted and I needed to convince her somehow to go back to her hotel room and rest. She yawned wide so I immediately seized my opportunity.

I stretched my legs out, "Don't fall asleep on me here, Hanson. I'm off the clock, remember? I'm not carrying your ass all the way back to the car."

"You ever think about coming back?" her head lolled on her shoulder in my direction.

When I turned to face her, I realized my arm was close enough to her that I could feel her warmth. Her hazel eyes stared into mine almost dreamily and I took notice of how close her lips were to me. I really, *really*, want to feel them on mine again. I had to fight the urge. I was a complication and she had enough of those already.

She pulled back slightly, "What are you staring at?"

Damn it, I've been caught.

"Noth...nothing," I shook my head and coughed.

Smooth. Real smooth.

I turned away again to refocus on the bubbling sound of the moving water when I heard Charlie whisper under her breath.

"Oh. I thought you might want to kiss me."

Chapter Twenty

CHARLIE

I can't believe I just said that out loud. But, I was throwing him a line and I really wanted him to take the bait.

I wanted something in this god-forsaken day to feel good or...normal and it felt good being with Eric. I wouldn't be able to count all the hours we spent here as children playing in this spot. Sitting with him now felt meaningful; for once my love life could be something but a complete disaster.

I mean, would it end up that way? Yeah, most likely.

It was hard being in a relationship with an agent. The long hours, the traveling, and the mostly soul-crushing caseload did not make good bedfellows with romance. And that's even before you add in the level of danger the job entails. Since my divorce, my average relationships have lasted three months at most. Although I did have one go for almost two years. But, I think that had more to do with his two six-month deployments on an aircraft carrier.

It was probably a dumb idea. Whatever sparks I felt last night were either imagined or extinguished. He couldn't possibly have held any attraction to me after witnessing not one, but two of my interactions with my moron ex-husband. I've found that most men were turned off by angry women with firearms and boiling aggression, no matter how justified it may be.

Shaking my head, I apologized, "Sorry. It was a stupid ide—"

Eric wrapped his hand around my face, pulling me into his own. His strong mouth was soft and experienced as it gently urged my lips apart. My eyes rolled as electricity shot through my entire body and his fingers stroked my cheek with every intentional wave of his capable tongue. He was slow and deliberate somehow knowing exactly what I liked and I felt my entire body responding in kind.

Wrapping my arms around his broad shoulders, I brought him down on me, never breaking our lock on each other. Running my hands through his hair, I wrapped my fingers in the dark locks and tugged gently. Our wet lips made a gentle sound when he pulled back and I opened my eyes. I watched Eric bite his bottom lip and seemingly squeeze his eyes in pain. When he finally opened them, he stared down at me and stroked stray strands of hair from my face.

"Something wrong?" I furrowed my brow.

He leaned down, kissing me long and lingering, but this time without his tongue, "No. It's perfect."

"There's a but," my hand landed on his jaw and I held it there.

Eric shook his head, "Only a small one."

"Which is?"

"I really want this Charlie. I want you. But, I want it the right way, you deserve that," he continued to gently caress my cheek. "I won't make the same mistakes with you. You mean too much to me."

"Eric...I'm not good at...relationships. Maybe we shouldn't get ahead of ourselves," I gave him a half smile.

His laugh was almost sardonic, "Yeah, me either. But, I want to try...with you."

Heat rose from the bottom of my boot-covered feet into my face. Euphoria spread over me like a blanket and I felt like a featherbrained school-girl. I was beginning to get used to the way Eric Tilset made me feel. Off-balance. Wired. Blissful.

In love?

Chapter Twenty-One

CHARLIE

The next morning, I found myself sitting next to Josie in the small office of Wyman's Funeral Home. It was what you could imagine when you thought of a small-town undertaker. A stark white building with neatly shuttered windows trimmed in black. The chapel, decorated in tones of mauve and pale blue, could seat around a hundred tightly packed visitors with a small overflow room next to the open vestibule.

Josie led most of the conversation and decision-making with the service director. I was mostly absent from their lives for a decade, so I was happy to have my cousin take the lead. I think it was something she needed also. Most of her life was filled with people making assumptions about her intelligence because of her condition. But Josie was not to be underestimated. Aunt Nettie raised her like any other child and never handled her with kid gloves.

It was at this meeting that I found out about my aunt's will. Nettie apparently prepared her daughter for her eventual death, telling Josie exactly how she wanted her service to be carried out and where to find all of her important papers. She had them in hand that morning including a simple handwritten will with the business card of a lawyer tucked inside. To my surprise, she left all of her possessions to me, not Josie.

That night, after dinner with Eric, I sat in my hotel room reading and rereading the three pages of her last will and testament. For the life of me, I couldn't figure out why she would have made the choices she did. I had abandoned them. I mean, it took my aunt dying for me to realize it, but that's exactly what I had done. Phone calls, cards, and flowers couldn't and wouldn't make up for not driving the two hours to see them for just one goddamn weekend. My stomach churned with guilt. I decided I would call her lawyer in the morning for answers.

Sleep evaded me, so when the neon red numbers of the hotel's digital clock switched to eight o'clock the next morning, I was already five cups of coffee into my day. I assumed I would get a paralegal or an answering service when the phone rang twice at the office of John J. Cooper, Attorney at Law, but Mr. John J. Cooper himself answered.

Okay, there may be some advantages to a small town.

Mr. Cooper advised me that he would be more than happy to explain everything after Nettie's funeral the next day, so we agreed to meet after the graveside service. I disconnected the line and my cell phone rang again immediately.

"Hello?" I refilled my cup a sixth time.

No answer.

"Hell-o?" I checked the caller ID, but it was no help.

Anonymous.

I pushed the red bar to end the call, but as soon as I did, *Anonymous* lit on the screen once more. I answered it again.

"Agent Hanson. Caller, are you there?"

I heard nothing but air before the line went dead.

Chapter Twenty-Two

DARKNESS

I heard the old woman died.

It was never my intent to kill her. She never should have been there! This is all my Dearest's fault though; they should have known better. I warned them. I warned them not to make me angry. Everything I've done for them has been for their own good. Why don't they see that I'm only trying to do what is best for them? For us.

The whore doesn't want my Dearest to see me, but I'm going to make everything right. Before long, my Dearest will see that I was right all along. There's nothing good that can come from associating with whores, even ones as good-looking as that sneaky slut.

Before long, I'll be the only one my Dearest can depend on.

CHAPTER TWENTY-THREE

ERIC

I pulled the car along the sidewalk in front of Nettie's home. Staring at the front door, I braced myself a little before exiting. This day would be tough for both of them, but I thought it may be worse for Charlie.

I knew she was probably feeling guilty for dropping out of their lives for so long. Charlie was a problem solver by nature. I knew others just like her and when they couldn't solve a problem, they ignored it. If she didn't visit the Falls, she wouldn't have to think about how much she missed her parents or the details of their accident. Out of sight, out of mind, as it were. But now, she would have to face the issue head-on because I knew she would never leave Josie alone in the world.

I rapped lightly on the plate glass of the front door of Nettie's Victorian home. I watched Josie's silhouette behind the curtain that covered the window make its way toward me. I knew it was her and not Charlie by her height. Her round blue eyes peeked around the fabric before opening the door wide.

"H...h...hi, Eric," she smiled, wrapping her arms around my waist.

"Hey Jos," I returned her affection. "You ladies about ready to go?"

Hearing the wooden staircase creak, I turned to see Charlie making her way down the stairs. Her dark hair was fashioned into a sleek bun at the base of her neck and she was wearing her black suit again. I offered to drive her to Seattle yesterday to retrieve more clothes, but she refused. I figured she was probably used to living out of a suitcase with her few handpicked items.

"I need to get my shoes on!" Josie turned quickly and jogged heavily down the hallway.

As Charlie came closer to me, I reached for her hand, "How are you doing?"

I played with her soft fingers and she gave me a half-hearted smile.

"I'm okay," she shrugged. "Have you heard from Bob Miller?"

I shook my head, "No. But, it's only been a few days. It might be another week before the fire marshal's report comes back."

She sighed. I knew what she wanted and I was doing my best to help her get it. Information and a lead. But, I was also afraid of what she would do once she had it.

"Charlie, I promise...we'll find out who did this," I wrapped my arms around her and pulled her close. Her intoxicating perfume of soft lilies and light musk filled my nostrils. I hugged her tightly, placing my lips against her forehead, "I promise."

She nodded, pulling away just as Josie returned with her purse in hand.

"I'm ready," she announced.

Charlie wrapped her arm around her cousin, "Me too, Jos. Me too."

Chapter Twenty-Four

CHARLIE

Eric, Josie, and I were the first to arrive at the funeral home. My cousin and I agreed along with the director that Nettie's casket would remain closed for the entirety of the services. The reasoning we discussed with Josie had more to do with being respectful of her mother's memory than allowing the public to see Nettie's horrific wounds.

It was bad enough that it was already Josie's last memory of her mother. I'll be damned if I'd allow her to relive it.

Entering the chapel, I gazed at the garden before us and was amazed at the amount of flowers that had been arranged and delivered in the past couple of days. I think every single person in Hydrangea Falls sent a basket, vase, or plant. Josie gasped and nearly ran to the front of the room where her mother's casket sat front and center.

"Look at all the flowers," she ran her fingers gently over a large container of pale peach roses.

Tears stung my eyes, but I fought against them, "I know Jos...aren't they beautiful?"

Eric must have noticed I was struggling and squeezed my hand.

Before long, a line of attendees formed, stretching out of the front door of the chapel and funeral home, and continuing down the sidewalk. I quickly realized how beloved my aunt was to this community. It made sense. She had worked the Rexall counter for more than fifty years. She watched generations of customers be born, reared, and have families of their own. I hadn't realized until I stood shaking hands with the multitudes of visitors that Annette Carter had been a pillar of this town and her death affected hundreds.

Guest after guest took their turns whispering their goodbyes as Eric, Josie and I stood near Nettie's casket as *The Old Rugged Cross* played overhead. It shouldn't have been a huge surprise to me when Audrey wrapped her arms around my neck, offering her condolences.

"Oh, Charlie," her weepy eyes glistened, "I am so sorry about Nettie. I just loved her! I remember us eating homemade ice cream out of those plastic pink bowls of hers on the back porch every summer. Do you remember that?"

My lips pursed in sweet recollection, "Yeah, Audrey, I do."

"I just can't...believe she's gone," Audrey dabbed her eyes with a tattered Kleenex.

I nodded.

"If you need anything...and I mean, *anything*...you call," Audrey slipped a piece of paper in my hand before looking shocked at Eric standing beside me, "Oh! Eric...you're here."

"How are you Audrey?" he asked politely.

"Well...I'm...well," she dabbed her eyes once more before scurrying to find a seat at the back of the busy chapel.

The service itself was sweet, short, and led by the Timberlake Baptist Church pastor Henry Simmons, a long-time friend of my aunt. It was everything I think she would have appreciated. I could almost hear her voice in my head saying:

"Child...don't you let them fuss over me."

Short and sweet was her style.

Eric, his oldest brother Bill, and four other men who knew, and loved my aunt, served as her pallbearers. A respectful hush fell over the sanctuary, as they carried her toward the large French doors. It was as I followed her casket down the aisle that I saw the sanctuary was standing room only. My heart swelled with pride for my aunt and then in an instant, a dark cloud of suspicion fell over me.

Someone here may know how and why that church burned.

Not now, Charlie.

The line of cars took nearly thirty minutes to make the two-mile drive to the cemetery for her burial. Again, Mr. Simmons said a few kind words about my aunt and how we can never know God's plan, but there was a reason why he took her and it was a blessing she didn't suffer.

I wanted to scream. I shifted uncomfortably in the folding metal chair next to her casket. I didn't give a damn about *God's* plan. Did *God* order the person to set the fire? Did he or she intend to murder my aunt and leave Josie an orphan? It took everything I had not to jump from that chair and storm off. How the hell could he know how much or little my aunt suffered?

Eric's hand under my elbow brought my brain out of its internal monologue. We were standing and shaking hands with the throngs of people once again offering their condolences. It was all too much. I had to get away from the social convention.

I leaned into Eric's shoulder, "Have to walk away. Stay with Josie?"

His brow furrowed with concern, but he nodded. I quickly made my way out of the open-air tent that was set up to offer shelter for the service and walked away from the crowd. The cloudy skies of late May threatened rain and I thought it might offer some sort of relief to the heated anger I was currently feeling. The tears I shoved off since that morning broke through my will and poured down my cheeks. It was uncontrollable and primal. I sobbed until my throat felt like it was on fire and I lost my breath.

"Ms. Hanson?"

A man's voice startled me from behind and I turned swiping the wetness from my face. Behind me stood a pole of a man with jet-black hair and steel-colored eyes. He looked to be around sixty years old with knobbing joints in his hands and sunkissed wrinkles.

"Yes. I'm Charlie Hanson," I wiped the final drops from the corner of my eye. The man reached out his hand, but when

I went to shake it with mine, he handed me a tissue instead. "Thank you."

He nodded, "Ms. Hanson, I'm John Cooper, Annette's lawyer. We spoke on the phone."

"Yes, of course, Mr. Cooper. Thank you for coming," I replied politely.

"You mentioned on the phone you had questions about your aunt's estate?" He prodded.

I nodded, "I guess I don't understand it. Why would she leave everything to me? Why not Josie?"

Mr. Cooper smiled a kind, grandfatherly grin, "Your aunt knew that her daughter, while very intelligent and independent, has her limitations. She didn't want just anyone, especially the state, to be granted guardianship of Josie. So, she left all of her retirement, savings, and stocks in a trust for her care."

I was frozen. Did he just say, guardianship?

"Whoa! Wait a minute. What do you mean... I'm Josie's guardian?" I was completely dumbfounded. It was as if I had been hit by a train. I couldn't be Josie's guardian. I had a life in Seattle and a career. Not to mention, I was determined to find out who killed my aunt. I couldn't be responsible for caring for Josie.

"I take it Annette never discussed this with you?" Mr. Cooper's face fell.

"Not a single word," I spat a little harder than I intended.

"I see. Well, Ms. Carter can be placed as a ward of the state if that's your wish—"

I shook my head, "No...I just. I'm sorry...I just need some time with this. How much care does she need? I mean...she lives on her own. She has a job."

"All true. But, Josie does have a heart condition that needs to be monitored and while she does pretty well keeping a small checking account on her own, her mother handled the bigger bills for her like rent and utilities," Mr. Cooper's tone was gentle. I don't know if it was the fact that my face went ghostly white or the sheer fear on my face that drew his empathy, but the kindly man continued without hesitation. "I understand you work for the FBI, Ms. Hanson. I know that most federal agencies have wonderful resources for caretakers of disabled family members."

My face twisted at the word disabled. I hated that word.

"Excuse me, my apologies...*differently*-abled," he quickly corrected.

I thought I might faint. I had absolutely no idea what kind of care Josie needed or even what a day in her life entailed. My brain was on fire trying to come up with any idea on where to begin. One moment, I was a single, independent, long-time divorcee, and the next, I was a parent to an adult daughter with medical issues.

I couldn't breathe.

"Ms. Hanson, can I get you a bottle of water or something?" he reached out his hand because apparently, he thought I might faint.

His concern was valid.

Shaking my head, I fought to grasp onto reality, "No...no, I'm fine. Is there anything else I need to know?"

He explained he had copies of all of Josie's medical professional numbers and her caseworker with the state at his office and invited me to stop by anytime as he would be more than happy to give me all the information I needed. I thanked him sincerely before we said our goodbyes and he made his way through the cemetery to his car.

I stood there watching the dwindling crowd of onlookers feeling nauseous. Eric saw me and headed in my direction. I didn't know what I would tell him or if I could tell him anything, since this wasn't his problem and I needed more information anyway.

"Everything alright?" he asked, concern shadowing his eyes.

I forced a smile, "Yeah...just...tired. I think I'm ready to go."

We turned just in time to see Audrey walking toward a disheveled-looking man in a crumpled suit. It was only as we got a few steps closer that I realized the man was Davy.

"What the fuck is he doing here?" my voice dripping with acrid anger. I started to charge toward him when Eric's gentle hand hung onto my arm.

"No...it's not worth it. Besides, it looks like Audrey is handling it just fine."

We watched as the woman shook her finger violently in my ex-husband's face. He said something then nodded twice and walked away.

"Huh. I wonder what she said...because apparently, my threats of jail didn't get the point across that he wasn't welcome," I snarked.

Eric never responded but shook his head as we headed back to the tent to find Josie.

Chapter Twenty-Five

CHARLIE

I waited until my aunt was in the grave twenty-four hours before I made the call.

"County sheriff's office. Officer Ed Walker speaking..."

I explained who I was and that I would like to speak to the officer investigating the fire at Timberview Baptist Church.

"I'm sorry ma'am...Officer Tweed isn't in the office at the moment. But I can tell you the investigation is ongoing and we will let the family know as soon as we know something concrete."

"That's not quite good enough," I interjected. "Then I would like to speak to Officer Tweed's superior."

Officer Walker choked a chuckle, "Ma'am...the Sheriff doesn't take direct calls from family members. Now, I understand that you just lost your aunt, but you're going to have to be patient and let us do our job," he placated.

All the professional niceties in the world weren't going to work on me today because I knew exactly what he was doing. I'm a master of polite deflection, but I would get some damn answers from someone.

Taking a deep breath, I cut loose on the unsuspecting man, "Look, Office Walker...don't make me go over your head or even the sheriff's head. I get that you're probably not used to doing any real police work in Hydrangea Falls, or anywhere in the county, for that matter. But, I will not sit on my ass while the person that killed my aunt gets away! Now, put me through to someone who can actually help me."

"I don't know who you think you are—"

"My name is Charlotte Hanson and I am a Special Agent with the Federal Bureau of Investigation. If you'd like to see my credentials, give me ten minutes and I'll show them to you in person."

He hung up.

Deciding to make good on my promise, I jumped in my car, heading for the Yamhill County sheriff's office. On the way, I reached out to Bob Miller, the fire chief. I didn't want to wait until Eric funneled any information to me, I wanted to hear it from the horse's mouth. I was avoiding Eric anyway. I didn't know how to handle a pending relationship since everything I had learned in the past twenty-four hours took the wind out of my sails. I wasn't being fair to him, and I knew it but he was unfortunately at the bottom of my priority list right now.

"Bob here!" the man's large voice bellowed.

"Chief Miller, Charlie Hanson...we met the other night at the church fire? Nettie was my aunt," I explained.

"Yes! I remember...how can I help you, Ms. Hanson?"

My car cruised into the parking lot of the sheriff's office, "I'm wondering if you've gotten anything back on the fire? Anything you can share? Off the record, of course."

"Huh...I guess you and the Probie haven't talked yet. I just got finished telling him that the preliminary report shows the accelerant used was pentane," he replied and I heard him rifling through paperwork.

"Which is what, exactly?"

"It's a hydrocarbon, like gasoline...not real common in the arson arena though," Bob explained.

Pentane should narrow the investigative scope significantly. Or so I hoped, "How would someone get their hands on it?"

"Internet, most likely. You can get your hands on just about anything there," he replied.

It wasn't the answer I was exactly looking for, but I thanked him for the update and disconnected our call just as I pulled on the door of the squat three-story brick building. I showed the officer at the door my federal ID and put my firearm in the bin provided before walking through the metal detector. He asked me to sign in and I obliged. I asked where I could find Officer Walker and he pointed me in the general direction of his desk.

Once in the open room of short cubicles, I noticed one nameplate read Walker and I made a beeline for it, but when I got there, it was empty. Turning to find someone else to help me, I watched a gray-haired man of around sixty walk in my direction.

Meeting him halfway, I held out my hand, "Hello, my name is Charlie Hanson. I'm here to speak with Officer Walker or Officer Tweed if you could point me in their direction."

"I know who you are, *Special Agent* Hanson," his lips pursing in a way that made me think he just ate a lemon. "I'm Sheriff Reeves."

I turned on my brightest professional smile, "Fantastic. I am looking for whatever information you can give me about the investigation of the church fire out on Timberview."

"I'm aware of what you want, Mrs. Hanson," he drawled through his paper-thin lips. "I can't give you anything."

I took a deep breath, "It's *Ms.* Hanson or Special Agent, sir. And you can't or won't?"

"Excuse me?"

"Can't is indicative that you *cannot* because you don't have anything. Won't means you either have a suspect or information that may lead to one and *will not* give either to me or..." I allowed my voice to trail off.

"Or?" he pushed indignantly.

"Or...you *will not* be investigating because it's not worth your time since you've already made up your mind on what happened and don't have the motivation to move further," I condescended.

His face turned violet with anger, "You little bit—"

"Neither gets me any closer to finding who killed my aunt," I interrupted, putting up my hand. "No need to answer... *Sheriff.*

I think I have a better understanding now...thanks for your time."

Spinning on my heel, I wove my way around the cubicles and out of the door.

When I got back into my car, I noticed two missed calls from Eric. I couldn't talk to him right now and I hated that I was shutting him out, but I had no choice. I just hoped he would understand.

Someday.

Chapter Twenty-Six

CHARLIE

The next morning, I made sure Josie ate a good breakfast before I drove her back to her apartment in Newburg. She was ready to go home and get back to her own life and I was happy to see her perk up after the last few days. There would be adjustments that would occur, but I was in no hurry to push her into anything.

As I made my way along the highway back to my hotel, my phone rang. I looked at the caller ID before answering and saw it was Eric. I allowed it to go to voicemail and then continued feeling guilty for ignoring him. I knew eventually, we'd have to have a conversation, but I just couldn't bring myself to have it just yet. Mainly because I still didn't know what I was going to say.

The phone rang again and before I could grumble about him calling again, I noticed the phone read *Anonymous*. I immediately picked up, "Hello?"

Silence.

"Look...whoever you are...it would be better if you spoke. I'd hate to run a trace on this number."

I looked down and the call disconnected.

This was the sixth crank call since Nettie died. One or two times I could blow off as a wrong number, but six? That's a significant pattern and just something else to add to the mountains of questions festering in my head. I drove the curvaceous highway in meditative silence.

The phone rang once more and this time I didn't look at the face of the phone before I answered it, "Ready to talk this time, asshole?"

Expecting dead air, I was surprised when I heard the voice of my boss, Bart Covey on the other end.

"Would you like to rephrase that, Charlie?" he asked carefully.

"DSAC Covey. Uh...I'm sorry...hello. What can I do for you, sir?" I stumbled over my words.

"Charlie, we need to talk. But first, how are you doing? I've been told you've got some added responsibilities now that your aunt has passed."

While we were part of a fairly close-knit team, I wasn't exactly accustomed to anything touchy-feely with my boss. It felt a little weird.

"I'm good, sir. I need to get some things set up for Josie before I come back...but I shouldn't be long," I cruised by my hotel, turning left to go around the block. If Covey wanted to talk to me, it was probably important and something I didn't want others to hear.

"Keep me updated...I've got some connections with resources that could be helpful. I also have a family member with the same condition," offered Covey.

I made another turn, still thinking about how odd this conversation was and a little stunned by his personal confession. "Thank you, sir. I appreciate that. Is there a reason you called sir? I mean...other than to offer condolences."

I heard him take a deep breath, "Actually, Charlie, there is. I received a call yesterday from SAC. Seems like you've been making some waves in your hometown."

"Sir?"

"Did you or did you not walk into the LEO's office and tell the Sheriff that your aunt's case was federal?" he demanded.

I slammed on my brakes, whipping into the parking lot of a McDonald's, "No, sir. I simply went to ask questions. That's all."

"Questions? Such as?"

"Sir," my voice tense, "My aunt was murdered. I think I have a right to find out who did it."

"Not as a representative of the FBI...you know that," he argued gently.

"Sir. I did *not* state that this was an FBI case—"

"Did you use your credentials to get through security?" he was interrogating me now.

I paused, "Yes, but—"

"This is not an FBI issue, Charlie. Stand down," he ordered.

I fumed. My aunt would never see justice if I couldn't get it for her and I certainly didn't trust the local sheriff's department to do a thorough investigation. I had to try harder.

"But, sir—" I pushed.

"No! Charlie. Enough. Don't contact the local LEO's again...let them do their job," he was quiet for a moment and when he spoke again, his voice softened. "Look, I understand where your head is at...but we can't just ride in like a bunch of cowboys and take over. Take care of Josie...I need your head clear when you come back."

"Yes, sir."

As I disconnected the call, large tears poured from my eyes. I wasn't sad, I was pissed. I pounded the steering wheel several times out of frustration. Covey was forcing me to give up and I didn't like it for a second but I also didn't want to lose my job. I threw the car into gear and went for a drive.

Chapter Twenty-Seven

ERIC

I pulled my sedan next to Charlie's. This girl was becoming an unpredictable mystery. She started distancing herself after the graveside services and had all but ghosted me now. I knew this game because I wrote the rules. But I wouldn't be like the women that had chased me, I would get an explanation.

I watched her from the driver's seat for a long moment before I exited the car. She stood on the bank of Broken Bow pitching rocks down the stream trying to get them to skip. Each time the stone would drop directly into the water with a large splash, but she tried again, one after another. I made my way over to her and stood silently watching for another moment.

"You need to angle your wrist parallel to the ground," I finally offered.

She didn't turn around, "When we were kids, I remember standing on the other side of this creek watching you and your brothers do this for hours. I never understood why. I get it though...it's therapeutic."

I moved in behind her, gently taking her right hand in mine, and directed her arm in the correct position. I pulled back on her wrist and she let go of the stone. It skipped across the water three times before finding its home. I pressed against her back, sliding my arm around her waist. Her body tensed as I turned her to face me.

"Eric. I...can't."

My heart crumbled into the ground beneath me. I knew this was coming, I felt it in the air. But until she said it out loud, I didn't want to believe it. This was my fault somehow.

"Why Charlie? Why does this have to be over before it begins?" My hand found her face and I held it. I searched her eyes for an answer but I only found them fighting with tears.

"Because things have changed. I have...different responsibilities. I can't do this now...I don't even know what my own life is," her voice shook.

"Charlie...don't do this. Please...I'm..." I knew I was losing the war. "You haven't given us a chance yet."

She pushed against me and put me at arm's length. I got the hint and I didn't fight it. I wouldn't invade her space.

"You need to go back to Las Vegas. Live your life...maybe one day we can...maybe not. I just can't right now," her voice was steady but the tears ran.

I was at a loss for words. This wasn't fair. She was shutting me out of her life and there wasn't a goddamn thing I could do about it. In one week, I learned that when Charlie Hanson made up her mind, there was no changing it. I backed away.

Our eyes remained locked on one another as I made my way back to the car. I opened the door but before I slid in the seat something came over me and for the fucking life of me, even to this day, I have no idea what made me say it out loud. But I did and I wouldn't take it back.

"I love you, Charlie."

Chapter Twenty-Eight
DARKNESS

Finally...My Dearest is all mine again. They will find out that I am the only one they can love...that they can trust.

I never liked sharing anyway.

From the moment we met all those years ago, I have wanted to be with them. We've always had a kind of connection that could not be undone. Every laugh, every gentle touch of our skin was like being in Heaven. Now we can be that way again.

This time, I won't let them go. It will be like it was. We will stay up late watching t.v. and eating popcorn in bed. We'll sleep until noon before starting our day and doing it all over again. My Dearest will finally smile again. And no one...not even the Whore...will come between us ever again.

I'll make sure of that.

CHAPTER TWENTY-NINE

CHARLIE

SIX MONTHS LATER...

"Hanson...Brent...Garcia...conference room two minutes," Deputy Special Agent in Charge, Bart Covey barked as he walked through the line of cubicles.

Jack Brent leaned back from his desk, rapping once on the short wall next to him, "What the hell's this about?"

My disembodied voice replied, "No idea."

The three of us promptly walked down the beige hallway, turning left into conference room A. We were met by Cynthia, an intelligence analyst with piercing blue eyes and curly black hair. She handed us manila folders filled with paperwork as we found seats around the large table at the center of the otherwise sparse room. Before we could open our documents, Bart's thundering voice filled the room.

"Alright...let's get started. What you've got in front of you is information regarding what the bureau is officially calling a serial arsonist. Behavioral analysis is still working up a profile, but they believe the person is employed...but he certainly has time to travel or travel as part of his job," he explained.

Jack cleared his throat, flipping through the brief, "What's he torching?"

"His pattern is odd," Cynthia replied. "But there have been two churches, a nightclub, and a couple of houses. The most recent was in Portland last week."

"Churches? Who does that?" Emile Garcia eyed the black and white photos. My gut panged, but I pushed the hurt away. Noticing my uncomfortable shift in my seat, he winced.

"Sorry."

"Any pattern to them? Same denomination?" I offered, ignoring his apology.

Shaking her head, Cynthia leaned in her hair, "No...one Baptist, one Catholic."

"So...not even in the same ballpark," Jack thought aloud.

"Precisely," Cynthia nodded.

"You three will join the task force already on the ground at the Portland field office. You'll have access to the investigative teams that are collaborating...read up on the local arsons here. They'll be expecting you at nine am tomorrow," Bart ordered.

"Really...joint task force now?" Jack groaned back at his desk. "I knew I should've put in for my vacation."

"What's wrong, Jack...you love Portland," I laughed.

Emile chuckled, "He's probably worried he'll run into ex-wife number two."

I roared with laughter because Emile wasn't wrong. Out of Jack's three failed marriages, the one with Scary Mary was undoubtedly the most contentious. She made his life a nightmare while they were married, but the divorce was a living hell.

Jack rolled his eyes, "Ha, ha...very funny. As a matter of fact...Mary and I are on good terms. It's Beth I'm worried about...I promised her this anniversary would be special."

"You're in so much trouble," Emile chortled. "I say start shopping for diamonds now."

Jack groaned.

Patting him on the back, I added, "Or a studio apartment...take your pick."

Chapter Thirty

CHARLIE

A chill wind whipped my light gray wool jacket as I and my team made our way through the glass doors of the four-story brick building off Cascades Parkway. Our trio landed in the city late last night and were just able to get a few hours of sleep and a cup of coffee before the early morning briefing. We checked ourselves in and made our way to a large area of the bullpen located on the fourth floor. We made it in just enough time to take seats near the back of the room before the meeting began.

After a rehashing of what we learned the day before in Seattle, the agent in charge, Phil Docker, moved to the head of the room to speak. A large man, Docker had a kind, wrinkled face that was made from years of happiness. I felt sorry for him in a way, he looked to be near retirement and should be done with a task force rotation. But I also understood that if he made it this far, giving the life up was something that was hard to do. Lucky for him, he was wearing a wedding ring and it looked old.

"I wanna thank you all for coming," Docker's voice was gruff; probably from an old pack-a-day habit. "We're putting you in two-man teams...each agent will be paired with someone from one of the local investigations to review evidence. We share what we have...go out...talk to witnesses. Let's hit the ground running and get this guy before someone gets hurt. A check-in schedule is pinned to the board along with team assignments."

I turned to Jack and Emile, "I'll find out who we're paired with."

I made my way through a few people who were standing alongside the furthest wall already discussing the case when I reached the large corkboard that was filled with messages, pictures, and updates. After locating the assignment list, I memorized Jack and Emile's partners before scanning for my name. It was then that I became aware of a large presence behind me.

"Hmmm...looks like I'm working with someone named Agent Hanson out of Seattle," the deep voice behind me said.

A singular bolt of electricity shot down my spine, making my knees weak. I knew that voice and recognized the sensation it gave. It was then I turned to look up into the face of Eric Tilset. I had a difficult time hiding the shock on my face.

"Eric! What are you—" I stammered.

His brilliant smile spread across his tan face, "Working...you?"

I blinked quickly, "You investigated these fires?"

"Yeah...I moved to the state fire investigation unit four months ago...right after the first hit," he explained. "But, you would have known that, if you ever used that email I gave you."

His familiar cologne filled my nose; pine needles and ocean waves. My heart was racing again, just being in his presence and it was incredibly distracting. I shook my head at him.

"What...email? You never gave me an email," I furrowed my brow.

"Huh," Eric twisted his mouth in thought, "I guess the heart was too subtle?"

I immediately remembered the tiny red origami he gave me the night of the reunion. I never thought to open it, not that I would have, because I didn't want it destroyed. I couldn't believe his contact information lived on my dresser this whole time.

"It's okay," he grinned. "But, it does look like we've been paired together...wanna find someplace to talk?"

Chapter Thirty-One

ERIC

The small coffee shop across the street from the FBI field office was bustling with customers as we took a seat at the tiny table in the corner. Charlie lifted the lid off her paper cup to add cream to the steaming contents and I watched her closely. My eyes followed her movement as they memorized every detail. Her hands seemed small but nimble and her neatly manicured nails only added to their gracefulness. Her woody hazel eyes were sharply attuned to their surroundings and finally rested on mine as I stared.

"Notice anything interesting?" She raised an eyebrow.

I smiled, "You like to watch the cream swirl to the bottom of your cup before you stir it."

Charlie pursed her lips. I knew she wished I would be serious. Our coffee date was of the professional variety, and not for pleasure. I couldn't help myself though, I was excited to see her.

"About the first fire in Vegas," she stated flatly.

"Of course," I cleared my throat. "The first one started as a result of gasoline and match...pretty common. It was the second one that was a little unusual."

"How?"

Opening a file folder in front of me, "This one took a little more finesse and, quite honestly, some ingenuity. Unlike the first, this one seemed to be a crime of planned opportunity."

I pulled pictures of a burned building out of the file and handed them to Charlie. She spread them out along the length of the table to look at them all at once. Her eyes quickly scanned each photo as I spoke.

"In this second fire," I pointed to the center picture, "You can see where the person used a piece of clothing as the timer. The first fire didn't use clothing but some sort of shredded plastic ball with handles."

Charlie continued studying the photos, "So, some sort of fabric soaked in gasoline? Was it something that they brought with them or found?"

"Most certainly brought to the scene for use in setting the fire, just like the first," I affirmed.

"How many of these are in Las Vegas?" she seemed to still be digesting the images. "Is that how you got involved?"

"How is Josie?" I smirked, taking a sip from my cup.

Charlie's eyes immediately met mine and she sighed, "She's good. She moved back into Nettie's house and found a job in Hydrangea Falls. We talk every Sunday and I make sure to drive or fly down at least one weekend a month. Davy is in jail again and no, I haven't been seeing anyone. Are we caught up? Can we get back to work?"

She stared at me but my smirk never relented, "That cute smile isn't going to work. Eric, this is business."

I knew it would work because seconds later, Charlie's cheeks flushed. Was I toying with her? Hell yes. I wanted her to admit that she made a mistake by not giving us a chance. Her admitting she was wrong was the least she could do after breaking my heart.

"Ask me," I sipped my coffee again.

She blinked, "Ask you. Ask you, what?"

"I know the question is eating at you. Just ask," I teased. Her cheeks flushed again. I knew Charlie Hanson well enough that she would want to know if I had been seeing anyone as well.

I hadn't.

"Fine. If we do this, can we then get back to work?" she placed both palms on the cafe table. I wanted so much to reach out and lace my fingers in hers. The urge to feel the electricity between us was overwhelming. I hoped she hadn't forgotten what it was like when we were together.

I shrugged, "Absolutely."

"How have you been?" she asked flatly.

My coy smile spread, "Well, after getting dumped by the most gorgeous woman in the world, I decided to reprioritize my life. I went back to Vegas for a couple of months then decided to move to Portland. I got a job in the state fire marshal's office."

I watched her body language relax and her face softened, "Oh. I didn't know that."

Shit. Now I feel bad.

"Yeah, well. You've had a lot going on in your life...I get that," I tried to backtrack my dickishness. She swirled the remnants of her coffee in its cup and avoided looking at me.

Charlie drank what remained, "Do you like it in Portland? Have you... been back to the Falls?"

I couldn't stand it any longer and I grabbed her hand in mine. It was warm and her skin was smooth like silk, "Charlie, I haven't been back since I left you on the bank of the creek that day. I wanted you to have your space...anything you needed. I'm being an asshole, and I'm sorry. We can get back to work."

I pulled my hand back but to my surprise, Charlie held on for a moment longer and squeezed my fingers before letting go. Our eyes met and hers held their smile for me. Maybe there was hope for us after all.

Chapter Thirty-Two

DARKNESS

I've enjoyed having my Dearest all to myself for so long, but now that the Whore is back, I'm not sure how long I can hold their attention. I went too far...

I wanted to tell my Dearest so long ago that I'm still here, I still care. They feel like they have no one, and that just isn't the case. How can I make them see that my feelings, my love is real?

I lie in bed at night pretending that I am near them. With every touch of my lover's hand, I close my eyes and imagine my Dearest is by my side. With every peck of my lover's lips, it's my Dearest that I feel. With every ember of desire in my soul, it's my Dearest that causes my flames to ignite.

My flames.

The flames.

My Dearest ignites the flames of my longing.

Chapter Thirty-Three

CHARLIE

His hand was warm in mine. I knew the instant he touched me, my muscle memory would take over. His strong arms holding me as we danced months ago at the reunion and the taste of his lips on mine were like haunting spirits in my mind. My stomach did its little flip like the first time, and like *every* time our skin made contact. His dark green eyes could read me like a favorite book and I knew he saw me blush.

I was too proud to say it out loud and in no way would I ever tell him, but there hasn't been a day gone by in the past six months that I didn't think about Eric Tilset. I played our last conversation, if you could call it that, over in my mind. It wasn't a real conversation by any stretch of the imagination, just me and my headstrong personality pushing him away. Most of the time, I questioned my sanity wondering why I didn't stop him. Why I didn't just let him in wholly, and fully into my life.

I'm a stubborn idiot, that's why. And while he sat here in front of me, teasing me with his picturesque good looks and that damn cologne he preferred, the one that drove me wild, I resigned to never being given that chance again. Realizing I was still holding on to his hand, I felt heat in my cheeks again and I cleared my throat, "So...the second fire. Clothing and gasoline as an ignitor...anything else?"

Eric immediately shook his head, "Not gasoline. Not in the second fire in Vegas, the two in Seattle, or the three in the Portland area."

He was handing me images as fast as he named the locations. I put my hand down on the photos of the fires I recognized occurring in Seattle, my city.

"I know these!" I said aloud to the shock of an elderly couple at a table nearby. I looked at them apologetically.

I picked up the first on the small stack, "This one was a gym where I used to work out. And this one is an empty brownstone that was under renovation in my neighborhood. I had no idea they were connected."

I studied the photo of the brownstone carefully. Every piece of wood was charred and broken. I could barely make out the once ornate banister attached to a now collapsed staircase. The railing looked like it had disintegrated with only a couple of blackened balusters poking up like burned toothpicks. It was lucky that one of the neighbors had been out walking their Shih Tzu that night or the fire would have spread to more homes, maybe even mine.

"So, this wasn't gasoline?" I quizzed.

Eric's face turned solemn, "No. We used a photoionization detector to investigate both the Las Vegas fires and the three in

Portland. But, because the VOC output wasn't exactly what we would expect with your run-of-the-mill unleaded fuel, we collected samples for further testing."

"Why do you keep saying three in Portland? I thought it was two. What did you find?"

It was bizarre to feel tension thicken between us and not in the *good* way you would expect. He was holding something back. I watched him adjust himself in his seat nervously and his Adam's apple move slowly as he swallowed hard.

He took a deep breath, "Pentane."

My heart raced so fast I thought I might vomit. It took all of my willpower not to completely lose any cool at the moment. Pentane wasn't a normal accelerant, Bob Miller had said as much months ago. Was it possible that the fire that killed my aunt and this new string of fires were connected? It could be a coincidence, but I didn't believe in coincidences, and neither did Bart. He ordered me six months ago to stay out of the investigation in Hydrangea Falls.

"It's not an FBI issue. Stand down, Charlie."

It was possible he knew of the connection. Was this his way of allowing me to get involved? I clearly had a personal stake in this case; maybe he didn't know about the unusual accelerant.

But as I said, I don't believe in coincidences.

Chapter Thirty-Four

ERIC

Charlie was anxious to immediately regroup with her team so we could all get on the same page. Although I didn't disagree with her, I was concerned that she may become more overzealous now that she knew about the pentane. I had to admit when the results kept coming in from each fire that it was used, I was a little taken back myself. Pentane is a saturated hydrocarbon that is both naturally occurring and a byproduct of natural gas production. It was highly unusual that it was used anywhere outside of industrial applications, especially on a trail of arson fires spanning less than a year.

The clouds billowed overhead and cold ozone filled my nostrils. I hadn't become reacclimated to brisk autumns that were common in the northwest quite yet and the building wind cut through my light jacket as we jogged up the stone steps of the federal building. I waited on the other side of the large metal detectors as Charlie checked her weapon and signed in. We rode the elevator together in silence as we made our way back to the fourth floor.

There were still several people milling around the room that was being utilized for this task force, but we made a direct line for the two men sitting opposite each other at a round table in the corner. The pair looked up as we approached.

"Hey Hanson, what's wrong? You look like you've seen a ghost," the man on the left commented. He looked to be around the same height as Charlie and spoke with a bare hint of a Spanish accent. The man on the right, who had his eyes on her from the second we set foot in the door, furrowed his narrow brow.

"She's got something big," he said.

"You guys spoke with Covey yet?" Charlie asked in hushed tones. Both men shook their heads.

"What is it Charlie?" the man on the right prodded. She motioned for me to take a seat then pulled one out for herself.

"Guys, this is Eric Tilset, the investigator for the Oregon fire marshal's office. Eric, this is Special Agent Emile Garcia and Special Agent Jack Brent," she motioned to the man on the left and then the one on the right.

I shook their hands, "Good to meet you. Eric Tilset, Oregon Chief Deputy Fire Marshal."

I glanced at Charlie as her eyes went wide. With my excitement at seeing her again, I had forgotten to mention my promotion. By the look on her face, I knew I would hear about it later. After we were all properly acquainted, Charlie turned back to her team.

"Eric and I have been going over the files from both the Nevada and Oregon incidents. We have an unusual pattern," she explained.

"Which is?" Jack pushed.

"The accelerant. In all but one of the fires, a chemical called pentane was used," she began spreading pictures from each fire on the table.

Emile studied the photos, "What the hell is pentane?"

"It's a hydrocarbon with a similar smell to gasoline. Highly flammable," I explained.

Jack returned to staring at Charlie. I didn't like him looking at her like that, but, I had no right to be jealous because we weren't together.

Yeah, keep reminding yourself of that, dumbass.

Jack's eyes narrowed on her, "Get to it, Charlie."

"Pentane is the same accelerant used in the fire that killed my aunt," she leaned back in her seat and I saw the lightbulb go on over her head. I wouldn't need to explain why I knew of three fires in the Portland area.

"What!?" Jack blurted hoarsely as Emile let out a low whistle.

Jack's eyes bounced around the images laid out on the table; he seemed to be looking for something, "Where are the photos and reports from the Seattle fires?"

The epiphany hit us both simultaneously and our eyes fixed on each other for a split second. The Seattle fires. Pentane wasn't the only thing connecting the blazes. Emile walked over to a nearby desk, retrieved a manila folder thick with paper, and returned to his seat.

Jack took the documents, "Thanks."

"What are you looking for?" Charlie leaned over to get a better look.

Jack pulled an image of what was left of the burned-out gym and held it out to her, "What is this place to you?"

"Her gym," I replied for her. Jack's eyes shot a quick glance at me then back to Charlie.

"He's right," she nodded. "I stopped going there right before that happened."

Jack shot another look at me that spoke volumes, something that didn't go unnoticed by Charlie.

"What? If either of you have something to say, then say it," she was getting irritated.

After a final side eye in Jack's direction, I faced her, "Charlie, there seems to be another connection...you."

Chapter Thirty-Five

CHARLIE

These men have lost their minds.

Right?

I can't be connected.

"Are you both crazy? No way," I shook my head defiantly.

Jack threw the picture of the torched gym at me, "Really? Are we crazy? Charlie...*your* gym. A house in *your* neighborhood. *Your* aunt's church. Take the blinders off, special agent."

Instead, I took a deep breath and sat back in my chair. Objectively, I could see where Eric and Jack were coming from, it did seem a little unusual on the surface. But, their theory didn't hold much water. There were two other fires in Portland and two in Las Vegas. The line didn't draw to me in those places, but I quickly realized it did to someone else; someone sitting at the same table.

Eric.

I dug frantically in the piles of photos that were now scattered between the four of us. I could feel three sets of eyes boring into me. When I found the one with an evidence sticker that read *St. Lawrence*, I plucked it from the mayhem.

I showed it to Eric, "Recognize this?"

Taking the picture, he nodded, "Yeah, it's from the St. Lawrence fire. The arsonist used their signature item of clothing and the pentane to set fire to one of the confessionals. Why?"

"What does it mean to you?" I led gently while searching for a second photo.

Eric looked confused and shook his head, "Nothing."

"What about this one?" I put another image in his eyeline. What used to be a house sitting on what looked to be a corner lot of a quiet neighborhood was nothing more now than foundation and ash. I felt my brain firing on all cylinders and the hair on the back of my neck was standing. I knew Eric was a piece of the arsonist's plan; I felt it in every bone. But, exactly what part he was playing, I couldn't answer. Yet.

"Charlie, what are you doing?" Jack put a hand over the messy stacks of pictures.

I cut my eyes at my partner, "I don't think I'm the only one being targeted."

"Okay...now who's crazy? Charlie, I don't attend church and I moved to Portland four months ago. I haven't lived here long enough to grow roots. I'll give you, it's weird that there have been incidents in Vegas and Portland, but until we learn differently, it's a coincidence. Plain and simple. They're both major cities...this guy probably travels. I think what we *can* agree on right now is you're our best lead," Eric stated emphatically with worry in his eyes.

Jack eyed us both, "Wait. What connection do you two have?"

"What?" I blinked furiously and looked like I got caught with my pants down.

Eric was more cool with his reply, "We've actually known each other for a long time. I'm from the Falls."

"Gotcha," Jack's word was sharp, and a smirk pulled at his mouth.

"Do you have anyone close to you that has a connection to all of these cities?" Emile rifled through the pictures.

"Yeah, him." I pointed at Eric.

His dark eyes rolled, "Other than him."

"What about Davy?" Jack wondered aloud.

I chortled, "My ex? No. I'm not sure if he's left the state of Oregon ever.

I couldn't imagine my idiot ex-husband being involved. It seemed a little too sophisticated for him. If he wanted to burn something down, he'd be more likely to use a bottle of Jack and a cigarette or be involved in a meth lab explosion. These fires seemed too planned.

"Why's he in jail this time?" Eric asked.

I shrugged, "I'm not sure. I've lost interest in the reasons anymore."

"I'll call over and get the details in the morning," Emile pulled out a small notepad from his pant pocket and began writing.

I knew my team meant well, but it was infuriating to think they believed I was connected somehow.

"Seriously?" I was exasperated.

"Charlie."

My eyes shot back to Jack as he spoke, "Let's get Covey updated. We can't do much more tonight...we'll pick this back up in the morning."

I nodded at my partner because I knew he didn't believe in coincidence any more than I did. I wouldn't let this go and he knew that much about me. I was sure that Eric was connected somehow; there was too much evidence piling up, whether they wanted to believe it or not. But what if my team and Eric were right? What if I was the link? The thoughts solidified in my mind. What if we were both not just connected, but targets?

Chapter Thirty-Six

ERIC

The skies exploded since we had entered the concrete edifice hours prior. Rain poured in sheets as I waited for Charlie to return from the ladies' room on the first floor. I was thankful when I remembered I parked in the garage beneath the building.

"Ahhh...damn it," Charlie looked out of the nearby doors as she put on her jacket.

I frowned, "What's the matter?"

"I forgot to call an Uber," she buttoned her coat. "And my umbrella."

I bit my lip. I wondered if I dared to offer her a ride. After my behavior at the coffee shop earlier, I didn't want her to get the wrong idea. I was done with making her feel bad over what happened between us. If we were ever to have a future, I wanted Charlie to be sure this time because I wouldn't be able to take another rejection from her. I wasn't going to get my hopes up.

I smiled, "Hey...no worries. I'll drive you wherever you need to go. You hungry?"

She eyed me, but to my surprise, it wasn't in suspicion of my motives like the way most women looked at me. It was almost as if she had been holding her breath all day and my offer gave her a sense of relief. Seeing her relax helped me to do the same.

I motioned my head toward the stairs, "C'mon. I'm parked in the garage."

The parking garage beneath the federal building was well-lit but could still make a person feel a little claustrophobic with its echoing low ceiling. We walked toward my truck, our footsteps bouncing off the mostly empty expanse. I hit the unlock button on my key fob as we drew closer which is when I heard Charlie giggling.

"What's so funny?" I asked as I opened the passenger-side door for her.

She stifled her giggles to an evasive smirk, "Nothing."

Once she was inside, I shut the door and jogged to the driver's side, sliding in behind the wheel, "Out with it Hanson."

Charlie unleashed a beautiful laugh that rang like a song in my ears. I hadn't heard that sound since the night we reconnected at our reunion. It was pure and it rolled off her like perfect waves.

"What?" I chuckled, starting the ignition.

"You can take the boy out of the country, but you can't take the country out of the boy," she was laughing again.

I eased my truck, my *new* truck, out of the spot and made my way to the security gate. I relinquished my ticket to the guard and he raised the barricade, allowing me to enter onto the street.

I finally turned to her, feigning offense, "Seriously? Making fun of a man's ride? How low will you stoop Charlie Hanson?"

***

I conscientiously decided that casual was the way to go. Once on the freeway, I headed in the direction of Portland's Pearl District. I knew of a couple of places where we could have a burger and a beer. Charlie continued her teasing about my driving such a large truck in the city, and I again pretended that my manhood was somehow damaged by her mocking.

We arrived at Timbercrew Brewing Company a little after six-thirty and within minutes, a very young hostess with giant brown eyes sat us at a high-top table near the bar. We flipped through the expansive menu before each ordering a cheeseburger, hand-cut french fries, and two dark ales. After the waiter dropped off our drinks we sat in weirdly awkward silence.

This is stupid. We're friends for fucks sake. Just talk to her.

There are times my inner monologue is more of an asshole than I am. But this time, I had to agree. We are friends and things shouldn't be this clumsy between us.

I took a drink from my glass, "So. Josie is good?"

"Yeah, she really is," Charlie sat her pint back on the table. "She misses Nettie, of course, but we're keeping her busy."

We're. As in *we* are. She said she wasn't seeing anyone; if that was the case, then who is the other person in *we*? Goddamn it.

I hated that I was analyzing every word that came out of her perfectly plump mouth.

"We?" I sipped my drink again trying to act uninterested. The corner of her lips pulled to one side in a sly grin. I could see she wasn't buying my act for a second.

"Josie's caseworker," she chuckled. "I told you, I haven't been seeing anyone."

I did my best to cover, "Oh...no, I didn't mean—"

Charlie laughed, "Tilset, why do you lie to me? Professional investigator and all. Besides the fact, you're terrible at it. "

"I'm sorry, Charlie. I'm really trying here," I took another pull of my beer. She looked around the busy restaurant uncomfortably, presumably to avoid any eye contact with me. I moved on with the conversation.

"Hey, I'm sorry back there in the bullpen...I didn't mean to catch you off guard with my role on the task force," I apologized. This seemed to alleviate some of the uncomfortableness.

Her eyes immediately locked with mine, "Yeah. Why didn't you tell me? That's a huge deal...congratulations."

I shrugged nonchalantly, "Thanks."

"Jesus, Eric. Don't you think I would have wanted to know about that? Or that you moved a thousand miles closer? You've been living three hours away for what? Four months?"

The more she spoke, the angrier her voice became. Before I could offer a retort or she could continue with her admonishment, our waiter returned with our meals and fresh drinks. The poor kid was good at reading his audience and didn't stick around to see if we needed anything else. As she arranged her burger with condiments, I volunteered an answer to what were probably rhetorical questions.

"Charlie, I didn't think you cared about any of that. Fuck, I haven't heard from you since the day I left. You have my number and my email...neither of which have changed. I get that you had a lot going on then...but after a while, you made a choice," I picked up several fries and shoved them into my mouth.

Her look was one of shock, but she didn't offer any excuses. We took our time picking at our food in pregnant silence. We both stared at televisions on opposing walls over each other's shoulders watching replays of the previous weekend's college football games. We were actively ignoring one another. When our waiter returned to offer more drinks, I asked for the check.

Our childish displays of obstinance continued into the short ride back to her hotel room. Both of us were too stubborn to admit that we had both made mistakes tonight. I pulled into an empty space at the Hyatt Regency parking lot and allowed the vehicle to idle. Out of my peripheral, I saw the contemplation on her face.

"Can you come up for a bit? To talk about the case," she picked up her messenger bag out of the floor near her feet.

I considered her question. Because of our own egos, we really didn't get to hash out why she thought I fit into the arsonist's motive. While I couldn't think of a single reason why this person, whoever they were, would be targeting me, the idea that Charlie had suspicions intrigued me. I shut off the engine.

Using her hotel keycard, Charlie swung the door open to her room on the eighth floor. Reaching inside, she flipped on the light switch before entering the room and then went inside. I followed. The room was pretty standard with a single king bed in the center, closet, bathroom, and a multi-function dresser-entertainment center-workstation combo. I took the office chair in the corner of the room as she unholstered her gun, placing it and the shoulder holster on the bedside table.

Charlie opened the mini-fridge, pulled a tiny bottle of vodka from the mini-bar, and tipped it in my direction, "Drink?"

"No. I've had my limit," I shook my head. She nodded, then emptied the bottle over a small glass of ice.

She took a sip, "Why is two your limit?"

I ran my hand through my hair. This wasn't the conversation I thought we'd be having.

"Well," I began, "I tend to get stupid after that."

Charlie pursed her lips, "What does that mean?"

Goddamn it. I really, *really* didn't want to have this conversation.

Just tell her, dumbass.

"Why does it matter?" I countered.

"Humor me," she rolled her eyes. Those gorgeous hazel eyes reminded me of quiet hikes in the woods around the Falls. Woody, crisp, and peaceful.

I leaned my elbows on my knees, hanging my head, "Charlie. There are things you don't know about me...things I'm embarrassed of."

I looked up to find her on the edge of the bed listening intently.

I sighed, "What the hell...okay. I went pretty wild in college and fire school. Drinking, partying, banging every woman who got my attention. Moving to Vegas didn't help the situation much. Or at all. I was always the guy looking for a good time."

"What changed?" Charlie sat her glass on the floor, leaning closer.

"The women got crazier and I got a guilty conscience. I don't know...I needed more. I wanted stability. So, I all but quit drinking. Stopped going to bars and stopped sleeping around," my voice trailed off. I was at a loss for something else to say or how I should explain my whole life. It was then I felt something warm on my clasped hands. When I looked up, I saw Charlie's hands covering mine.

"You..." her voice was barely audible even in the stillness of the room. "You really meant what you said, didn't you?"

Floods of memory rushed over me. That day on the bank of Broken Bow; the last time I saw her.

"Every word," I whispered.

CHAPTER THIRTY-SEVEN

CHARLIE

I rose from my seat at the edge of the bed, and Eric backed further into the armless leather office chair to give me space. I didn't need or want it. I knew this wasn't the right time, but I needed to be near him. I didn't allow his gaze to move from mine as I took a small step on either side of him and straddled his lap. Wrapping my hands around his neck, I pulled my hips squarely onto his.

"Charlie—"

I wouldn't allow him to protest and I put my lips on him to keep any from escaping. My kiss was slow and deep. Running my hands through the longer hair on the crown of his head first, I worked my way down. I could tell he had recently gotten a haircut as the close crop around his ears felt like velvet under my fingertips. I ran my tongue over his teeth as I released his mouth. I opened my eyes to find his squeezed together in agony like the time we kissed at the edge of the creek.

"Is my kissing really that bad? You're gonna give a girl a complex," I whispered, still rubbing his freshly clipped hair with my hands.

Eric never opened his eyes, but smiled a soft grin, "On the contrary, I don't think I've ever had one better."

I smoothed my hands over his five o'clock shadow and kissed his lips again gently. I wanted him to look at me or touch me but his hands were holding onto the seat of the chair. I was getting emotional whiplash at this point as his signals were really like riding a rollercoaster. One minute, he's flirting and the next he's an iceberg.

"Will you look at me," I pecked his lips again, "please?"

"Charlie—"

"Eric, please," now I was begging.

Finally relenting, he let out a short sigh as his lids slowly opened. I didn't know what I expected to find when he looked at me, but it wasn't the rims of redness that I saw. He looked like he was fighting some intense emotions and I leaned away to get a better look.

"What's wrong?" I asked.

He rolled his eyes indignantly, "I can't do this, Charlie. I can't."

"Do what? Kiss me?" I furrowed my brow.

"Exactly. I just...can't," he stated firmly. I thought he might push me off his lap for a split second to get some space, but he didn't. He just stared at me, his eyes daring me to spur on the conversation.

Or, at least that's what I was telling myself. I didn't want to believe the small voice in my head whispering to me he found someone else. He grilled me for information on my personal life, but I never reciprocated. Maybe I didn't want to know, because I knew it would hurt. He could very well be in a relationship with someone here in Portland and be very happy with her. I would be happy *for* him.

"So, you've got someone. That's great...I mean, I'm happy for you. Really." I lied through my giant lying, liar mouth. I was not happy. I was quickly getting angrier with myself as the seconds ticked.

What an idiot. You missed your chance. And now, you've made a fool of yourself.

Eric's muscular jaw set in a hard line, "No. No, Charlie...I don't have anyone. I haven't..."

His body tensed and the heat that emanated from him was like waves on summer blacktop. It didn't take any of my FBI skills to know he was pissed. I watched him, waiting for him to continue.

"You don't get it," his eyes locked with mine. "Please get up."

I moved off him and he immediately jumped from the chair, making his way to the door.

"Hey! Talk to me! Help me understan—"

He whirled on me with concentrated frustration, "I meant what I said! Every word, Charlie! I haven't been with anyone since I left you in the Falls. Don't you get it? I love you, Charlie!

I love *you*." Pausing, he whispered under his breath, "Goddamn it."

I stopped cold in my tracks. I must have looked like a deer caught in the headlights of his truck because the acrimony immediately melted from his face. He took a small step closer to me, lowering his voice.

"There is *only* you Charlie. If I can't have you then I'd rather be alone. I'm not saying that to garner your affection...I'm just telling you how I feel. But what I can't do is let you break my heart again, even unintentionally," he took another step and he was close enough that I could smell the pine and ocean waves. His large hand brushed my face, "So, no, Charlie...I can't kiss you or allow my skin to touch yours and it not mean something. And I won't apologize for that."

A lump was growing fast in my throat. I knew months ago that Eric loved me, but I somehow allowed it to fade from my thoughts even though I felt the same way. When I ran into Eric at that reunion, I had decades of walls built around me. I wore unbreakable armor and my heart lived in a house of ballistic stone. Somehow, in a very short time, he tore it all away. I allowed my fierce independence and ability to meld into my current situation, rebuild those barriers around me, and disguise my feelings. It was as if I was watching my future disintegrate before my eyes.

I opened my mouth to speak but before I could, the window of my hotel room exploded.

Chapter Thirty-Eight

CHARLIE

I latched onto Eric's hand, and yanking with all my weight, I pulled him to the floor.

"Get down!" I screamed. Crawling on my belly, I made it to my nightstand and pulled my Sig Sauer off the tabletop. I turned back to check if Eric was okay and found him flat on his stomach staring at me.

Two more pops rang out and the sound was deafening.

I clambered over him, keeping my chest tight to the ground. I knew the buildings' concrete facade and internal wall would offer enough protection and the shots didn't sound like a large enough caliber to break through anyway. I squatted on the balls of my feet with my back firmly against the outer wall, then quickly shot a glance out of the empty frame where my window had been seconds earlier.

I half expected Eric to freak out yelling at me and demanding to know what I was doing. To my surprise, he instead watched every move I made and emulated them exactly, making his way to the opposite end of the enormous, missing window.

He peaked around his corner just as I had, "What do you see?"

"Nothing," I shook my head.

The little light the parking lot offered and the heavy rain obscured most of what my eyes could adjust to. I heard the sound of screeching rubber on the wet pavement just as I poked my head out once more. I barely caught the taillights of a late-model sport utility vehicle crossover. One of those cars that were a dime a dozen on every street, in every city, in every state.

"Fuck!" I dropped my gun to the side. Almost immediately, heavy bangs beat on the door.

"Charlie! Charlie! Are you in there? Are you alright?"

It was Jack.

I lowered my weapon again and stepping over and through shattered glass, I let him inside, "Yeah, Jack...we're okay."

Jack stopped short when he saw Eric then holstered his gun. My partner never said a word, but his face spoke volumes. I knew he'd give me shit later.

"What the hell happened?" Jack looked around at the scattered shards of glass covering every inch of my room.

"Well, either we're getting too close or," I snarled as I scooped up my belongings, "I might have a target on my back. Either way...I'm pissed. Where's Emile?"

"Downstairs. He'll handle the locals when they arrive. You got what you need? We better get back to headquarters and get a statement from both of you," Jack replied.

I took a quick look around and noticed Eric already had the duffel containing my personal items and my work bag in hand.

I strapped my weapon back to my side and grabbed my jacket before heading into the hallway as the wails of sirens moved closer. Our trio avoided the elevator, instead, opting for the eight-story jog down the stairwell. As the fire door opened, the scene at the front desk was a cacophony of excited voices and flashing lights.

I watched Emile nod in our direction indicating we were clear to return to the federal building. As we made our way through the parking lot to the stereotypical, standard-issue, black SUV, I turned back to the hotel and groaned.

"What's the matter?" Eric threw my bags in the back seat.

I sighed, "I was really looking forward to soaking in that big tub."

CHAPTER THIRTY-NINE

DARKNESS

The Whore and my Dearest are up to their games again! I cannot allow the Whore to sink its claws into my Dearest. My Dearest is weak and easily fooled by people like the Whore. The Whore is cunning and will use whatever means necessary to lure people into their trap.

I cannot allow it to happen again.

I need to reevaluate my plans. So long have I wanted my Dearest by my side...ever since that night and my eyes gazed upon their pure beauty once again. Memories of our time together is the only thing that keeps me fighting.

I will burn the world down to be with my Dearest once more.

The Whore has no right to them. It's my turn to show my true love how much they mean to me. My past gifts of passion haven't been good enough. I must prove that we, my Dearest and I, are meant to be for eternity. In this life and the next.

In this life and the next.

Pure until eternity.

Chapter Forty

ERIC

After arriving at FBI headquarters, both Charlie and I rehashed and retold our version of events no less than fifty times while leaving out the more personal details from the night. Jack and Emile were incredibly thorough asking the same question ten different ways only to come up with the same answer as the first nine. There came a point when their investigation felt like an interrogation. But, I couldn't hold it against them, someone took a shot at a member of their team. *Someone* tried to kill Charlie.

My blood boiled.

It was around two in the morning when Charlie slipped in the door of my interview room. With her back pressed against the frame, she quietly watched me. If she wanted to continue our conversation from the evening prior, I would stop her cold. My brain was running at a hundred and I was entirely too wired to have a heart-to-heart. It would have to wait for another day.

"The guys are just finishing up the paperwork," she pulled out a chair to sit across from me.

I nodded, "Good. I might actually get a solid thirty tonight." She smiled.

"You still on the case or are they sending you packing?" I lifted my chin toward the door.

I had a feeling that the greater majority of her time in a room like this was spent persuading someone in charge that she was still capable of participating in the task force. I didn't know a lot about how this agency worked, but I had to assume that whoever was responsible for her would want her safe, and right now it didn't seem like that was the case.

"Still here... for now. We've got to make some headway soon...this guy is getting damn bold," she replied then yawned.

I looked at her concerned, "Where are they putting you up at now? Surely not the same hotel."

"No...I'll find something else. Or I'll hit the rack here," her mouth gaped again.

The door swung wide and Emile stood in the doorway, "Hey Eric...sorry it's taken so long. You're free to go. Looks like we're all meeting back here at nine am...sound good?"

I slid the metal chair back to stand, "Great. Thanks, man."

With a nod, he was gone leaving Charlie and I alone once more. I found my way to the open door when she stood in front of me.

"Eric?"

I looked down, meeting her gaze. I wanted to do so much more and if we hadn't been standing inside a room that I'm certain wasn't exactly private, I would have. I wanted to wrap my arms around her and tell her how absolutely terrified I had been tonight. I wanted to hold her against me and swear that I would find out who fired on us in that room and make them pay. I wanted to protect her.

"We'll talk tomorrow," is what came out of my mouth. I pulled her into me and hugged her tightly and she returned my hold. We stood in each other's warmth for a few short moments. Before breaking away, I kissed her head.

"Tomorrow."

Chapter Forty-One

CHARLIE

By the time I got myself checked into a new hotel room, one on the opposite side of town and closer to the Portland field office, I barely had enough time to grab a nap and a shower. While my snooze was short, barely an intermission to my day ahead, it was productive. When I arrived at the office, I immediately began combing over old cases looking for someone who might have a grudge against me and could also reasonably get their hands on the pentane.

Eight forty-five and six cups of coffee into the day; that had to be a record.

I got up from the desk I was borrowing for the time being and stretched. I made my way back to the coffee maker and met Jack pouring himself what I could only assume was his first shot of caffeine that day.

Amateur

"When did you get here?" he poured an illegal amount of sugar into his paper cup, stirring it with a tiny plastic straw.

Adding a splash of cream to my cup, I watched the clouds billow, "Early."

I glanced at my partner over my mug as I took a sip of the steaming brew. He was staring at me as if he were waiting for me to finish my story.

"What?" I quipped.

Jack, never one to beat around the bush as it were, stopped mixing the contents of his cup and began chewing on the straw, "You gonna tell me what the deal with you and the Fireman is?"

"Nothing," I replied, turning my back to him and returning to my desk. I heard Jack laughing behind me as he followed.

"Jesus Christ, Charlie! Are you seriously pulling that shit with me?" He sat on the edge of the workspace still chewing on the drink stirrer. He leaned in, "I saw the way he looked at you...there's history there."

I rolled my eyes and Jack choked back more laughter, "I knew it! So, who is he, Hanson?"

Jack wasn't going to give up. After working with him for the past five years, I knew that much. He would escalate the snide comments until I punched him in the face or told him about Eric.

I opted for the latter.

"Alright...alright. Eric's an old flame...we grew up together. Neighbors, actually. I ran into him about six months ago at my high school reunion. Remember when DSAC ordered us to take time off?" I explained begrudgingly.

"When your aunt died?" Jack furrowed his brow.

I nodded, "Yeah, Eric...was a comfort. And yes, we got *close*."

An impish grin was fighting taking over my partner's face, "I bet he was."

"Jack."

He put his empty hand up, "Sorry...I'm kidding. Wait." His face fell serious, "He was there when the fire at the church happened?"

I nodded, "In town? Yeah...like I said, we were at the same reunion that night. He met me at the hospital."

"Charlie!" Jack's face was contorting into disbelief. "Did you question *how* he knew?"

It was then I noticed another figure standing just within earshot of our conversation.

It was Eric.

Chapter Forty-Two

ERIC

"As a matter of fact, she did ask me," I stated flatly. I knew what Charlie's partner probably thought because I could objectively see it from his perspective. To him, I was a stranger, a mere vagabond wandering my way through his turf.

I got closer to the pair, "I carry a scanner with me all the time. It's always on."

The pair stared at me blankly before Jack raised an eyebrow.

"I find it oddly comforting. Anyway, that's how I found out about the fire at the church and Nettie. Look, I've been a firefighter for more than twenty years...and I know why you would think that about me. But I didn't do this. If my superior or anyone else suspected me in any way, I wouldn't be here." I didn't enjoy defending myself, but in this case, I would be understanding.

Charlie raised her eyes at her partner as if to say in my defense, *"He's right."*

"My apologies," Jack replied sincerely. "Look, I'd be a shitty agent if I didn't suspect everyone."

"And a shitty partner if you didn't suspect those closest to Charlie." I put my hands up, "No worries. I get it, I do."

He took the last sip from his cup before tossing it into a nearby trash can, "Round table in ten."

I watched Jack walk away slowly. I understood he wanted to protect his team, but he was barking up the wrong tree if he thought I had anything to do with the fires or what happened in the hotel last night. My eyes eventually floated down to Charlie's as she watched me watch Jack.

"Did you finally get settled in?" I cleared my throat.

She nodded, "Yeah."

I opened my mouth to ask how she slept, but she cut me off.

"I'm getting more coffee...see you in a minute."

Her demeanor was a little more icy than it had been a few hours prior. I was wondering if I missed something. I thought over the past twenty-four hours. Admittedly, it had been a long day, but for the life of me, I couldn't think of any reason that would cause her to be so short. Except—

I waited for her to walk by me on her way to the meeting and grabbed her arm. Her woody eyes narrowed on me.

Lowering my voice, I leaned into her, "Lunch? Just you and me. Someplace quiet."

She nodded.

I released my gentle hold on her arm and followed her the rest of the way. The walls of the room containing the round conference table were covered with images of the fires. Starting as soon as you walk in the door, on the left side of the room, a record of the known events has been created. None of the images were new to me, except that there seemed to be an addition to the official timeline.

Making my way to that side of the table, I gazed at the pictures that were added. My heart sank when I saw the familiar burned remnants of Timberview Baptist Church. The FBI had made their decision that the fire that killed Nettie Carter was connected to the rest. I felt terrible for Charlie. Would they take her off the case now? Her boss was pretty direct with her back in May; no way was she to be involved in her aunt's accident. I resigned to the fact that it was a good sign she was still here.

I didn't sit next to her like I had the past couple of days or like I wanted. We chose seats across from each other, narrowly missing each other's glances over the space. The group, made up of Charlie, myself, Emile, and Jack also included two local agents, a forensic psychologist, and a supervisor from my state fire lab. We examined pictures, discussed the movements of the perpetrator, and established a travel timeline, all while considering the new addition of Nettie's murder and the shooting at the hotel the night before. What we didn't talk about out loud, but what was becoming clear was the idea that someone from Charlie's past seemed to be who we were looking for.

After three hours of repeated discussion, Jack finally put a lid on the boiling pot, "Alright, I think we all need a break...let's leave it here and meet back tomorrow."

He was met with nodding and softened murmurs of grumbling agreement. Charlie and I rose from our seats simultaneously. She tossed her head to the side as if telling me to meet her out of the conference room and away from prying ears. After giving those around me cordial goodbyes, I headed for her temporary desk. I only had to wait for a few seconds before she was standing beside me.

She picked up her messenger bag, stuffing files inside, "Lunch then?"

Chapter Forty-Three

CHARLIE

I'm not sure what I'm supposed to say to him exactly. We walked silently down to his truck in the parking garage and when he opened the doors for me, every door, my voice caught in my throat. Even saying a simple thank you was lost. I was struggling to be around him. We weren't able to finish our conversation last night, but an attempt on your life pretty much puts a full stop on everything.

He headed south seemingly taking us back downtown, but after leaving the busy midday freeway traffic, he was moving down side streets leading through beautiful and quiet neighborhoods. After a few more turns, he eased the vehicle into the driveway of a small craftsman's style home with white wood siding. The swooped peak of the roof and arched porch entry created a quaint and inviting look. Turning in my seat, I knew my expression spoke before I did.

"Where are we?"

"I promised you a quiet lunch. This place has excellent prices and the service is next to none," he smiled, sliding out of the truck. I followed him onto the small stoop outside of the arched front door.

"This is your place?" I quizzed as he punched in the code to the electronic lock. He smiled again, opening the door for me.

"After you, Agent Hanson," his hand motioning for me to enter ahead of him.

Inside, the house was warm and intimate. The cozy living room, painted a soft white, offered a plush olive green sofa, simple, but tasteful decor, and a large flatscreen television mounted over the fireplace. The room flowed directly into a small, but tidy eat-in kitchen with a built-in bar that separated one room from the other. Suddenly, I felt something brush against my leg and when I looked down, I saw the dark, silky body of a cat weaving between my feet.

"Oh my! And who are you? The hostess?" Bending, I plucked the young feline from the floor and it purred loudly. I raised a brow at Eric.

He scratched it between its ears, chuckling, "This is Pip. She's my roommate...and an all-around bed hog."

"Pip?" I held the lanky cat to my face, gazing into her jade-colored eyes. She purred louder. Eric tossed his keys on the counter of the bar and pulled open the refrigerator.

"Yeah," he shrugged. "Like Pippin Took? It's a character in Lor—"

"Lord of the Rings, yeah, I know," I laughed. "You poor thing... your dad is some kind of nerd."

It felt good to laugh. To joke about something so trivial. And Pippin, who was now snuggled in my elbow, was quite the stress reliever. I watched Eric remove meat, cheese, mayo, and bowls from the refrigerator. I cradled Pip like a baby, smoothing my hands gently over her soft face as I paced. Her whiskers twitched and she seemed to smile as I stroked her, eyes still closed.

"This is a great place," I did my best to make conversation but meant every word. His house was beautiful.

Eric worked at the counter, putting sandwiches on plates, "Thanks. The backyard needs some work still...I'll get to it eventually."

He set the two plates on the tiny table nestled in the bay window of the kitchen then added silverware, glasses, and napkins. He invited me to sit.

"You'll have to put her down, but lunch is served," he smiled.

I deposited Pip on the sofa and she looked up at me, yawning. Washing my hands at the kitchen sink and then turning back to the table, I saw Eric waiting for me with a chair pulled out. While I'm not a woman who expects special treatment from anyone, I am also someone who spends all of her waking time wading through criminal scum and fart jokes with my mostly-male teammates. Chivalry was always a pleasant surprise in my daily life.

"Thank you," my voice finally offered as I sat. Eric took the chair next to mine and I looked at the delicious spread of food. "This looks fantastic."

He offered a quick nod, "No problem. I hope smoked turkey on sourdough and Caprese pasta salad is okay."

"I'm excited it didn't come from a vending machine or drive-thru," I laughed and he laughed with me.

"I guess you don't get to cook a lot, huh?"

I took a bite of my sandwich. The bread had the perfect texture of crunchy crust and chewy body; it was heavenly.

Shaking my head, I swallowed my bite, "Not at all. I guess I'm used to it though. It's just me anyway."

I put a fork full of the pasta in my mouth; the fresh basil and tomatoes exploded with flavor. It was legitimately so perfect. I frowned at him.

"Did you make this?" I asked. He smiled, covering his full mouth with a napkin and taking a second to swallow.

"You sound surprised," he chuckled. "Pasta salad and bread aren't difficult."

Pursing my lips, I stared at him for a moment, "Well, aren't you the perfect man."

He raised his eyebrows but continued chewing his food. I immediately felt tension between us and realized I crossed an invisible line.

Goddamn it.

I know we needed to talk about the night before, and I have never shied away from a difficult conversation. But with Eric it was different. I gave a damn what he thought; about me, about us, about everything. I have sat across from some of the most disgusting and deranged individuals known and haven't felt as apprehensive as I did at this moment.

Taking a deep breath, I put my hands in my lap, "So, we came here to talk."

Eric took a moment to finish his bite of food before turning to me.

"I'm sorry."

"For...what?" I frowned. I know my face screamed confusion because that's what I felt.

"For being an asshole...for...treating you like shit. For not insisting you stay here last night," he put his napkin on his near-empty plate.

"What are you talking about? I think I should apologize. I'm sorry I crossed...well...*trampled* a boundary last night. And you have no obligation to take me in. I'm fine at the hotel," I countered.

I was not going to allow him to think that because he spoke his mind to me last night, his feelings weren't valid. I had done a lot of thinking myself, which, if I'm being honest, was the real reason I didn't sleep. I needed to make sure what I knew to be true in my heart was also reconciled in my brain. I needed to be real with myself. For a split second, when I thought he had someone else, I was jealous and...broken.

Eric shook his head, "I know you don't need it or want to hear it, but...I should have protected you last night. I should have insisted you stay here...in the spare room if you were more comfortable. Anything to make you feel safe."

His comment should have made me cringe; I mean, I'm the one with the gun. But, it came from a place of sincerity not a caveman mentality. I quickly realized Eric was the only person I would allow to protect me outside of my team.

"It's okay. Really," I gave him a small smile. Eric stared at me for a long moment. I could tell he wanted to say something else, but he was searching for the right words and I was completely empathetic to the feeling.

Eventually, he worked it out and he took a deep breath, "Charlie...can I ask..."

Another sigh.

"Where are we going? I mean...last night, before all hell broke loose, you seemed to...you know. But this morning, I'm getting a brick wall. I just need to know that we have a chance. Or..."

"Or..?" I paused. "Look, Eric...it's complicated. I'm complicated, so, I'm sorry if I'm not on your timeline."

Indignant shock fell over his face, "My... timeline? I don't have a timeline, Charlie."

Rising from the table, he snatched his plate, dropping it into the empty sink. Pip jumped at the sound but quickly snuggled back into her spot.

"You know, you're not the only one with a complicated love life in your past. I'm no angel. And when I went looking for something more...it took me years to find it. But, that arrow Cupid shot me with came with strings, didn't it?" he charged.

I felt my jaw set and the anger building, "Strings huh? Well, telling me there are conditions to our relationship won't cut those strings any faster. Eric...I don't even know if I can do what you want. Jesus Christ...I married the first person that asked and look where that led. I've not had a relationship last more than a few weeks. If I'm lucky...I might get a couple of months. One time...I got two years...which was a record."

"Charlie...I just want to know if we have a shot. That's all. I just want to know that you're ready and willing to *try*. That's all I want! That's all I've ever asked. Just for you to try," his rising voice took a dip, becoming more calm.

Walking over to me in the middle of the living room, he hesitantly took me by the arms, "I'm sorry about Davy. And every other guy that couldn't handle all of who you are. Your career, your life...your walls. But I'm not those men...I just want a chance to prove to you that you and I are different together. That maybe...the reason nothing has worked for either of us, is because we didn't have each other."

His forest-green eyes looked into mine and it felt as though time stood still. I felt every emotion I had ever conceived about him consume and dominate me. I sensed my armor shattering as I stood in his gaze. I could not ever deny, from that moment forward, that every piece of my soul belonged to Eric Tilset. I knew he felt it also because he leaned his lips within centimeters of mine.

"I...I want..." he whispered as he placed his mouth on mine.

Rockets exploded in my head and my core quaked. With each passing movement of our lips, our bodies were more entwined with each other. His powerful arms engulfed me, lifting me off the hardwood floor. I would surrender my mind and my body to him now and forever. We both made the choice then that our souls were inseverable.

Chapter Forty-Four

ERIC

I never wanted to let her go.

I felt the moment her walls came crashing down and she finally allowed me fully into her world. Her mouth was full of a tangible sweetness that I wanted to take a lifetime to explore. I wouldn't push it too far because I wasn't that guy anymore and she was worth the wait.

My hand slid down her side onto her waist when I felt the vibration. Cradling her head in my other hand, I pulled away from our kiss, "I think it's for you."

Groaning, her hazel eyes rolled in irritation, "Damn it."

I gave her a little shrug and smiled. We would have a lifetime of interruptions and we would have to get used to it. I recognized why other men would find a relationship with Charlie difficult. She was driven, career-minded, determined, logical, and stubborn. All things that would intimidate weaker men. I am no weak man which is why I've seen her passion, compassion, softness, and her heart.

"Hanson," she answered abruptly. Her eyes bounced, actively listening to whoever was on the other end. "Yeah, yeah, no...he's right here. Okay, we'll check it out. Oh, really?"

She shot me a sly look. "Okay, thanks, Emile."

"I guess I should thank you," she purred, sliding her phone back into the pocket of her navy suit pants. She wrapped her arms around my waist.

I frowned, "Why would you thank me?"

"Emile got your delivery. But if we were having lunch, why didn't you just have them sent here?" she stood on the very tips of her toes to peck my lips.

What the hell was she talking about?

I pushed her back gently, "Charlie, send *what* here?"

She fell back on the flats of her feet, staring at me.

"The flowers?" She looked at me like I was crazy.

I heard the words she said but not their meaning, "What flowers? I didn't send any flowers."

She scoffed, "Eric, c'mon. There's a giant bouquet of lilies and chrysanthemums at my desk right now. Just like the ones you sent after you left the Falls."

My heart was racing as I fought to find a logical, non-homicidal stalker reason for what she was telling me. Biting my lip, I shook my head at her in dissent, "Charlie...I didn't send you flowers. Not back then, not today. It wasn't me."

It was the first time I saw real fear wash over her face, but it only lasted a second as she was quick to regain her composure.

In her eyes, I watched her sharp mind think through scenarios rapidly. It took her a minute before she spoke again.

"So you didn't send me flowers," she confirmed, I was sure for her own satisfaction.

"No," I replied firmly.

Her eyes widened again, "Eric. That first bouquet was sent to Netties...not my hotel room. Whoever this is has to know about Josie."

I watched panic and unadulterated fear come in waves in her eyes. Josie was the single most important person in her life. A threat to her was like threatening her own daughter.

"Charlie, look at me. No one is going to hurt Josie. Hey!" Grabbing her shoulders I forced her to look at me, "Are you hearing me? We're going to get this bastard."

She nodded and a light went off in my head. Returning to my kitchen, I grabbed my phone and flipped through the contacts.

"What are you doing?" Charlie followed me.

Finding the person I wanted, I hit the send button and waited for an answer, "I'm going to make damn sure no one gets close to Josie."

Ring number one.

I needed someone on the inside that no one in their right mind would mess with: Brooks Hernandez came to mind. Standing nearly six feet, six inches, the former Marine was intimidating, to say the least, and was a monster of a man. Brooks and I were friends almost as long as Charlie and I, but we kept in touch a little better over the years.

Ring number two.

This is how I knew after twenty years of service, Brooks moved back to the Falls with his wife and four children to make a home and begin his second career in law enforcement. The last time we spoke was three months ago when I congratulated my friend on his promotion to Chief of the small, but mighty, Hydrangea Falls police department.

Ring three and the line comes alive, "Hey! Tilset...good to hear from you."

"Brooks! Hey man...how's it going?"

CHAPTER FORTY-FIVE

ERIC

There was no way that I would allow Josie to be in danger. After explaining the situation to Brooks, he was more than happy to accommodate my request for help. I also called on my brother's wife, who knew Nettie and Josie, to stop in every couple of days. I would have all eyes in the Falls watching her and luckily, my plan helped Charlie relax a bit.

Under her insistence, we were already back on the road early that afternoon heading toward the Northwest Regional Computer Forensics Laboratory, or RCFL, to meet with Dana Brenner, an FBI computer analyst. While I worked on securing Josie, Charlie had gotten herself busy tracing the origin of the mysterious flowers.

After convincing the local florist who made the delivery to allow a specialist to take a look at their computer system, Charlie reached out to her colleague. My luck was still holding enough to find a place on the street in front of the large, nondescript building, and Charlie quickly paid the meter before we went inside.

The receptionist, an older woman of close to sixty with a sweet smile, walked us back to Dana's office. After announcing us, she turned on her heel and left. Dana rose from behind a laptop and an otherwise extremely spotless desk, "Charlie! So good to see you."

She shook Charlie's hand.

"And this must be?" she held her hand out to me.

"Eric Tilset, Deputy Chief Fire Marshal," we shook hands. She motioned for us to take a seat.

I was a little taken aback by our host. She was much younger than I imagined an FBI agent to be and she looked like she came straight out of the pages of Vogue magazine. She was tall, blonde, and carried the delicate form of someone who lived on caffeine and not much else.

"Dana, thank you so much for meeting with us so quickly. I know you're busy," Charlie leaned her elbows on her crossed legs. "Did you find anything?"

Dana raised her eyebrows, "I might have something. It looks like your mystery flowers were ordered via a web-based proxy server. Now, the thing is, those types of servers aren't always the most trustworthy and are pretty easy to track."

"How easy?" I pressed.

"Well, *easy* is a relative term," she pushed her thick, black-framed glasses further on the bridge of her nose. "It's an anonymous server...meaning it's made to keep information like this out of anyone's hand. But, as it turns out, I'm great at what I do."

Turning the laptop on the desk around, Dana pushed the machine toward us so we could watch a recording of keystrokes.

"Here," she pointed at the screen, "I'm back-tracing the blocks here and swimming through the proxy's code."

She paused.

She pointed at the screen again, "And here is where we find the IP address of your admirer."

She beamed at us like she was expecting praise or a pat on the head. Charlie and I glanced at each other. I wasn't sure what she was thinking, but I was ready for the supermodel to tell us what she found and stop giving us her resume.

"Dana...what exactly does this tell me? I can't exactly knock on the door of an IP address," Charlie huffed.

"I can tell you that this person is in Portland and they're most likely staying in the Doubletree right over here by Holiday Park," she shrugged.

"What!?" Charlie nearly came out of her seat. She was excited but agitated at the same time. But, then again, having a maniac send you flowers would put anyone on edge.

She turned to me, "It's less than a mile from the Hyatt to that hotel...maybe a couple minutes drive."

I nodded, remembering the black SUV from the night prior. Someone could easily have made it back to the Doubletree before any police arrived on the scene; they would have just blended into the rest of the traffic. The planning of the shooting was meticulous. I was betting they didn't expect her to have company, however.

We stood to leave.

"Dana, thanks so much. I'll keep you in the loop about a warrant...we may need you to come with us," Charlie reached to shake the woman's hand.

"No problem!" she replied with a go-team attitude. "I hope you catch this guy soon...I wouldn't want any more of those creepy flowers delivered to me."

Charlie stopped. Turning back, she tilted her head oddly at the agent, "What do you mean, *creepy*?"

Wrinkling her nose, Dana looked like she was sucking on sour candy, "I saw what he purchased. Lilies and Mums? I don't want to freak you out, but can we say funeral flowers?"

The looks of bewilderment were plain on our faces because she continued like we were clueless.

"Lilies and Chrysanthemums?" she urged trying to get us to understand something we couldn't. "You apparently know nothing of floriography."

We continued to stare at her blankly.

"The cryptological study of flowers as a means of communication? You know...like red roses represent love...an iris symbolizes hope...stuff like that," she explained finally. I nodded sharply in hopes she would spill the beans faster.

She didn't.

"So? What do those specific flowers mean?" I snapped, but she didn't seem to notice my impatience.

"Death."

Chapter Forty-Six

CHARLIE

The cloud-blanketed sky grew darker as the sun set somewhere beyond and the streetlights were already illuminated by the time Eric and I walked out of the RCFL. I needed to give the information that Dana assaulted my mind with a minute to marinate. Some psycho, who has been following me around for months, tried to kill me last night and then sent me flowers representing death today.

I've never claimed my life was boring, but now I wish it were.

I needed time to think. There had to be someone in my past who had the means to pull all of this off. Was it Davy Wyatt? That thought crossed my mind for a fleeting second but it took less time to leave. Davy wasn't near smart enough or even had the guile to do it. Besides, according to Emile, he was still doing a year's stint in county jail. However, it was clear that I would need to go through my old case files again; the thought of which lay heavily on my shoulders.

It was a lot of cases.

I was silent as Eric drove us across town back to headquarters. Lost in my thoughts, I barely noticed when he pulled into the parking garage below the building. Grabbing my bag we started for the elevator when the doors opened and Emile strode out.

"Did you get my special delivery sent over for prints?" I called out as we got closer.

Flipping his key ring around his index finger, he grinned, "Yes, boss. But you know they won't find anything."

Boss. A term of endearment between us and the same nickname he calls his wife.

"What are you two up to now?" Emile asked.

"I'm going to look over my case files again...there has to be something there. Something I'm missing," I readjusted the shoulder strap of my bag. "Jack still around?"

He tossed his head toward the low-hanging ceiling, "Still up there. I'm just going out to grab a bite...Need to call Gloria."

"Okay...tell her hello from me and we'll see you in a bit," I pushed the button on the elevator.

"Yup," Emile turned to walk away.

It was then that the roar of a fast-moving motorcycle filled the compact space. The rumble of its engine bounded and bounced off every surface as it howled closer. We could hear it was coming with some great speed and the three of us turned to see it racing down from the second level. As it neared us, the dark-clad driver lifted an arm and I felt Eric's full body crash into mine as we crumbled to the concrete.

Three shots rang out as we scrambled to find cover. I heard the throttle on the bike open up as I sprung out of Eric's grip with my Sig in hand. Bolting after the driver, I ran as fast as I could pulling the trigger four times at their back. The motorcycle turned a corner speeding out of sight.

"Charlie!" Eric's bellow echoed off the walls of the garage.

I glared in the direction of the bike, but turned back, running toward the sound of his voice. Re-holstering my weapon, I turned the corner where the elevator was located to find Eric's bloody hands ripping open Emile's blue Oxford shirt.

"Oh my God! Emile!" I slid like a runner to home base.

"Help me put pressure here," Eric ordered, shoving his jacket in my hands. His voice was steady and had a calm reserve to it, forcing me to focus. I needed to not think about who he was working on, just that I needed to help.

"Are you still there...?" a distant woman's voice asked.

Eric pushed his phone with his pinky where I could see it, "Yeah, we're here. What's the ETA on that bus?"

"They're en route...two minutes out," the voice replied.

The elevator doors made their familiar ding. When they opened, eight agents barreled out, weapons drawn. I looked down into Emile's face as it turned a ghostly white. I realized then that there was also a large gash near his temple.

"Eric," my voice shaking, "his head."

Ripping the bottom half of Emile's open shirt, Eric shook his head, "I'm getting to it. I'm not seeing an entrance wound...I think the bullet just grazed him."

I swallowed hard.

In the near distance, we could hear the wailing of the ambulance getting closer. I looked down at my colleague and noticed a soft gurgling emanating from his chest as I also felt another presence standing over us.

It was Jack.

"Why does he sound like that?" I whispered.

Eric's face was grim, "I think the bullet hit his lung. Here...take this and apply pressure to his head, I've got this."

I moved to Emile's head and lay the torn piece of the shirt on his temple, applying pressure. The cry of the ambulance siren was deafening as it drove into the garage.

Immediately, a crew of two paramedics jumped from the cab of the rig with response bags in hand. Eric and I moved out of the way as soon as they knelt down next to Emile.

"GSW to the left lateral thoracic cavity and left temple...possible pneumothorax," Eric reported as he stood. We backed away, allowing the medics to do their job. I felt a firm hand on my elbow. Turning, Jack was still standing behind me.

"What the hell happened?" he barked.

My head shook, "I don't know. One minute we were standing here talking...then this motorcycle came out of nowhere."

"Fuck!" snarled Jack. "And you didn't see anything? No plates? A driver? Anything?"

"Hey!" Eric stepped between us, "Back off."

My eyes whipped at Eric, staring him down. I didn't need him defending me to anyone, especially my partner. I knew Jack was scared, and so was I. He was lashing out at the situation and not me. I knew that. If Eric and I were ever going to work, he would need to know where the line was and not cross it.

I raised a bloody hand at him, "Stop. Please let me speak with my partner. Alone."

Eric and Jack's eyes were locked on one another but Eric finally turned back toward the paramedics as they secured Emile on the backboard. Jack watched him until Eric turned away.

"Who does that guy think he is?" he barked hoarsely.

"Jack, let it go. Look," I stepped in his eye line of Eric and Emile, "that bike didn't have a plate...and the rider was dressed in a black leather jacket, pants, boots, and helmet. I got four shots off—"

"Did you hit him?" he broke in on my sentence.

"I don't think so, but the techs need to look for a blood trail," I replied, pointing in the direction the assailant took.

"West exit?"

Nodding, I turned to see the paramedics loading Emile in the back of the ambulance. I watched Eric's face as the doors shut. He looked worried. The ambulance's siren wailed as the driver romped on the gas leaving the garage.

I looked around at the chaos surrounding me. It was almost like someone had slowed down the videotape on the TV as more agents and crime scene techs poured out of the elevator. I barely noticed when the crime scene tape was strewn and markers were laid where shell casings fell; my eyes stared at the pool of Emile's blood.

"Hey," Jack touched my arm, "Go to the hospital...Covey will have called Gloria by then. She's going to need a friendly face."

Scowling, I protested, "Absolutely not. This is my case, Jack...this guy's after me. No one's benching me. I'll tell Covey that myself."

Now I was pissed.

"No one's trying to bench you, Charlie. We need someone there when he comes out of surgery...please, Charlie," he pleaded with me.

"He's right. C'mon...I'll drive," Eric was at my back.

I pursed my lips. I didn't like being ganged up on, which is what this felt like.

"Fine. You get any leads...Jack, I'm your first call," I narrowed my eyes on my partner.

He nodded, "My first call."

CHAPTER FORTY-SEVEN

DARKNESS

*T*he Whore has been warned.

CHAPTER FORTY-EIGHT

ERIC

The air behind the automatic doors of Legacy Emanuel Hospital was warm as it hit us in the face. Charlie flashed her badge at the nurse before engaging in a brief conversation with the older woman. I knew she was on edge, so I waited a few feet back to give her some space. After finding the coffee machine I fed a couple of wrinkled dollar bills into it and watched the steaming brew drip into two cups.

I found Charlie using wipes, presumably from the older nurse, to clean her hands. I realized suddenly that I was a mess too.

I sat the cup in front of her, "It's hot...not sure you can call it coffee though."

"Thanks," she continued wringing the towel through her hands. I sat next to her and watched as her scrubbing became aggressive and desperate.

"Hey, hey...stop! They're clean," I put my hand over hers. She sighed heavily.

We watched the hands on the large clock hanging above the waiting room door tick by for two hours. Just as the hand hit hour three, Jack and two other agents found us and took up the vigil. By hour four, we had a stack of coffee cups ten high and were just about ready for another round when a middle-aged man with salt and pepper hair wearing green surgical scrubs entered the room.

"Garcia family?" he eyed our wearied, motley group.

Jumping from her seat, Charlie was quick with her "Yes."

We gathered around the man, Dr. Diallo, as he explained Emile's condition. While the bullet was removed from his chest without much incident, he would have a chest tube to remove the air from the cavity. All seemed well until Dr. Diallo explained that Emile was not out of the woods as he was experiencing some mild brain swelling from the graze to his temple. His team placed the agent under a medically induced coma for observation. The next few hours would tell them if Emile would suffer permanent damage or not.

I kept a close eye on Charlie the entire time. All color drained from her face and I watched the tears welling in her eyes. She fought them off until a tiny woman with jet-black hair and matching eyes appeared in the doorway.

"Gloria," Charlie's breath caught in her chest as the held tears finally fell.

The group of agents surrounded the small woman as Dr. Diallo ran through the series of events once more for Emile's wife. As one would expect, she cried and shivered with sobs. Jack put his arm around her for comfort, but it was in Charlie she sought her refuge.

"Oh, Charlotte," reaching up, Gloria wrapped her arms around her neck.

I have been a firefighter for a very long time and this was the first time I witnessed grief from this side of the fence. It was also the first time I had ever heard anyone outside of Charlie's family call her by her birth name.

Charlie sobbed, "Gloria, I am so, so sorry. This is all my fault."

The modest woman immediately released Charlie and grabbed onto her shoulders in what looked like a death grip. Gloria's eyes were hard as steel and her lyrical voice firmed quickly, "You listen to me...I will not hear anymore of that. The person that shot my Emile? It's *his* fault. Do you understand me?"

Charlie nodded.

Gloria patted Charlie firmly on the shoulders, "Now, you will come with me to pray the rosary over him...then...you will find the bastard."

***

The floor of the Intensive Care Unit was quiet and the waiting area more spacious as the group of agents and I watched through thick glass as Emile's wife, Gloria, prayed at her husband's bedside. She held her beads and Emile's fingers in one hand and Charlie's hand in the other. Charlie's eyes were closed but I could see she was still fighting the tears from falling.

I saw her eyes open, presumably after Gloria finished, and she hugged the woman. When her gaze met mine, I knew she was exhausted. As she exited the unit, we waited with breath held until she spoke.

"Jack...Gloria said you could come in now," she said hoarsely. He brushed past her only stopping for a moment for his large hand to pat her on the shoulder. She never looked up but stood nodding her head stoically. She walked toward the elevators and I followed silently.

It was morning again but the thick clouds covered what would have been a beautiful sunrise. Pigeons cooed overhead as I followed Charlie to my truck. Unlocking it unprompted by her, I took a deep breath before I took my seat behind the steering wheel.

After sitting quietly for a moment, I finally turned to her, "Where to?"

"My hotel. I need to change...into what...I have no idea. Everything I have is filthy," she sighed.

"Why don't I take you home?" I offered quietly.

Her eyes rolled in my direction, "Really Eric, I don't think I'm in the mood."

I paused.

What kind of guy did she think I was?

"No, Charlie. Your home. In Seattle. We can pick up a refresh for you," I cut my eyes in her direction.

I was annoyed. I understand that I've been a self-proclaimed womanizer in the past, but I haven't been that man in quite a while. I certainly wouldn't take advantage of her, or anyone for that matter, when they are as emotionally spent as she is now. I reached for my pack of cinnamon gum.

But in my next thought, I realized we were both probably feeling the effects of adrenaline leaving our bodies and exhaustion taking over. I suddenly understood that I needed first to check my own emotions and remember that she was hurting. Charlie just prayed over a member of her team. She was spent. Shoving the stick of the sweet and spicy confection into my mouth, the hair on the back of my neck prickled and I realized she was staring at me.

I glanced in her direction, "What?"

"You would do that?" her voice a lot less venomous than before.

"Drive you to Seattle? Of course," I affirmed, pushing the gum to the back of my jaw. Her ginger eyes examined me for a minute.

"I think I have some joggers at the hotel. I'll pay for breakfast on the way."

CHAPTER FORTY-NINE

CHARLIE

I threw my keys into the bowl sitting on the table next to my front door. My body felt numb and dehydrated and for a moment I forgot why we had driven the three hours to my apartment. Trauma is a marathon, but I was comforted when I felt Eric's hand on the small of my back.

"Nice place," he smiled.

I gave him a weak grin, "Thanks."

He looked around, noticing my sense of style was not unlike his own. My living room was cozy with space for an overstuffed sofa and a chair. The lamps on the side tables, that I had on timers, created a soft, golden light that added to the room's warmth, and a small bookshelf, filled to bursting, rounded out the space.

"I'll be just a minute," I sighed. "There's water in the fridge...or you can make coffee. Help yourself."

I felt a wave of empathy wash over when Eric looked at me. It was difficult seeing Emile's wife pray her rosary at his bedside. And I'm sure it was just as hard watching me as I secretly prayed as well. Emile is a good man and the person responsible for putting him in that coma would pay.

I left Eric in the living room to trade out my dirty clothes for clean. I was thankful that I at least had the shirt and sweatpants I was wearing since everything else I had taken to Portland was either torn, sweat-stained, or covered in blood. I found myself staring into my bathroom mirror without a thought of how I made it that far. There was still a small drop of blood on my ear. I touched it and heavy tears fell from my eyes. I stood in the mirror watching myself cry.

I couldn't stop the salty drops from streaking down my face as I sobbed in the bathroom alone. I felt all the pain in the past six months I constantly shoved deep inside, now spilling over. Nettie. Eric. Emile. It was all leaving me en masse as I bawled. Eric must have heard the sniffling because when I looked back into the mirror again, I was startled to see his muscular frame filling the doorway. I didn't move.

From the moment Emile was shot, Eric tried to keep his distance from me. That's what I *normally* would have preferred. I would want time to analyze and consider the situation. But somehow, at this moment, he sensed our foolish tiff was over and I needed him. He cleared the space between us in two strides, pulling me into his chest. I didn't resist. Instead, I melted into his embrace.

"Shhhh," he soothed. "It's okay, baby...it's gonna be okay."

My head shook, "None of this is okay, Eric."

I know he agreed with me that nothing about what was happening was right, just, or fair. His offering was a moment of comfort and solace. Looking down into my eyes as they overflowed with tears, Eric brushed the escaping droplets from my cheek. His hand was like velvet on my face as he moved them over me, and I leaned into his touch as he worked his way into my hair. He cradled my head in his hands as he slowly pulled our lips together. His breath was sweet as he inhaled mine, and he seemed to pull my essence further into his being.

I didn't refuse him but joined him as our mouths danced with one another. Weaving his fingers in my hair, he held my head steady as he moved down my neck with his lips. Unable to hide his yearning, he pressed into me and allowed me to feel his immense excitement.

My hands grasped onto his shoulders, fingernails and all, and he moaned as I dug into him.

"Charlie..." my name dripping from his mouth like nectar.

Releasing his hold on me, Eric caged me between the vanity counter and himself with his mountainous arms and towered over me as his body pressed harder into mine. I would let him have me on the countertop if he wanted. My hands found the waistband of his jeans and I pulled at his belt to free him of his constraints. I wanted him, *all of him*, and our pasts and egos be damned. I tore at his shirt and buttons flew in all directions, making little pinging sounds as they hit my tile floor.

It was the first time I really had a good look at his body. Eric always carried an athletic-type build, but over the last two decades, he had bulked up a good portion of muscle. I knew now that it wasn't just his charming personality that drew women to him. It was the broad pecs, the rippling six-pack, and the three beautiful tattoos on his right shoulder, bicep, and inner bicep. The largest is a black and white firemen's shield with the words *duty, honor, trust,* and *integrity* on each of the cross's four wings. I marveled at the gorgeous piece of artwork as my fingertips traced its outline.

Tilting my head up towards his, Eric kissed me hard and long. His mouth still tasted sweet from his gum.

Without removing his dewy lips from mine, he swept me off the ground. He wrapped my legs around his hips and I clung to his hard body as he carried me toward my bed. Never unlocking our lips, he sat me gently on the edge as he slid his hands under my tee shirt, lifting it and my bra aptly over my head. I felt exposed and suddenly shy at the moment as I realized it had been years since I had been intimate with anyone. He gazed hungrily at me and immediately my brain forgot all about restraint and was begging for him to devour me.

I wrapped my hands around his hardened abs and kissed his navel. My fingers shook anxiously as they worked to finish ridding him of his pants, but his erection made my task difficult. Anticipation consumed me as I stripped what remained of his clothing until everything finally fell in a heap at his feet leaving all of his length revealed. My groin throbbed.

He bent toward me, his mouth exploring mine as he guided me back toward the large mound of pillows bordering the head of my king-sized bed. His large hands cupped my body. When he reached my hips, Eric's fingers hooked inside my joggers, peeling them away. His hands continued to run along my calves, softly inspecting every inch of my frame. My center glistened with expectation and I moaned softly in delight. I wanted him to take me then.

"Er-ic," I whispered, reaching for any part of him.

Still working his hands along my thighs, he delicately opened them wider, exposing all of my essence. He made small purrs of delight as he gingerly laid kisses over every tingling mound and crevice. His strong tongue expertly released a river of passion from me and my back arched in pleasure, as I floated on clouds of elation and euphoric bliss.

No man had ever made me want them, *need* them like I needed Eric Tilset.

The feel of his body on mine sent sparks of pleasure exploding along my spine. It had been more years than I wanted to admit since I had been with a man and my legs quaked with anticipation. He was anything but just *any* man. He was a god, my life-saving Prometheus of the modern age.

Gliding his way up my body, his erection grazed my entrance and I quivered. Running his tongue over the mounds of my breasts, they too reacted to his touch. His body on mine was electrifying as if our very nerves were connected. Eric found my mouth once more while continuing to caress my hills and valleys until he again encouraged fountains of honey with his fingertips. I wanted to offer him my release but not before I felt him inside me.

"My god, Charlie...I need you," he moaned desperately in my ear and his breathy voice sent gooseflesh racing along my neck.

I bit his ear playfully, "Then what are you waiting for?"

"Permission," he breathed.

All I was giving him wasn't enough. He needed me to consent to his desire.

I reached down, finding his hardened length, and guided him inside me. I cried out his name as he drove into my core. I felt the pressure inside me building and I almost couldn't wait for its release as he set his cadence. My back arched again as I let out a primal scream of pleasure as the bed rocked violently. Bright lights flashed in my eyes and I saw my entire existence with him, beginning to end, past, present, and future, flashing in front of them.

My entire body vibrated.

My climax urged him deeper into my center and his rhythmic movement launched us both further into white-knuckled ecstasy. Beads of sweat formed on Eric's brow as his stride became faster and our hips made thunderous claps together. We were one.

Wrapping my legs around his perfect ass, I drove him deeper with every motion. Groaning, his eyes rolled and he bit his lip. Bending his back like a contortionist, Eric thrust his shaft deep and he bucked wildly as he reached the apex of his climb.

His bellows of pleasure filled my ears and the room around us.

Chapter Fifty

ERIC

My entire body shook and my arms were quivering as I pulled Charlie's nude body against me and we panted in unison. Charlie pulled a downy throw blanket from the edge of the bed, tossing it over us.

"No," I pulled the blanket back, exposing her gorgeous form. "I'm not finished looking at you."

Color flushed her cheeks but I didn't care; she's beautiful. Her ivory skin was flawless and perfect even with the few battle scars she carried. My fingers trailed along its silkiness creating a glow of gooseflesh in their wake. I realized that I could die in this moment knowing I lived a good life. Charlie and I were finally where we were supposed to be. She rolled to her side to face me and it was then that she realized I was still staring at her.

"What?" she smiled blissfully.

Licking my lips, I paused for a moment, "You are beautiful. I mean...you've always been pretty...but—"

My lips engulfed hers. She tasted delicious on my tongue and I was ravenous for her, like a starving man consumed with his first taste of bread. And she had other areas I couldn't wait to taste again.

"You're beautiful," I pulled away, shaking my head as if trying to clear the cobwebs from my mind. I stroked her cheek with my thumb, drawing her face closer to mine for another, softer kiss. "I love you."

I watched the tears return to her eyes. It tore at my soul to see her crying because I knew her pride but this time, she surprised me with a soft smile.

"I love you too."

My heart stopped and a lump formed in my throat. My brain instantaneously exploded with possibilities of my future with her. She was my all and her declaration of those four little words set me ablaze.

I rolled her over onto her back, stroking her valley once more until it gave up its fountain of sweetness. I was ready for her to be wrapped around me again but not until I heard her shout my name to the heavens. There was almost no need for me to dive into her paradise because I was almost to the point of no return without it. But with her last cry of my name, and to my surprise, she rolled on me and mounted my shaft deep inside of her.

Her Valkyrie form was angelic above me. Locking her eyes on mine, she set a quickening pace that had me vigorous with excitement. Her gaze never left mine as I thrashed, easily reaching my climax and her name spilling from my lips as I quaked from the aftershock.

She climbed down, trying to pull the blanket over us again. I again pulled it back, this time tossing it to the floor and panting, "No way, Charlie Hanson. I've waited my whole life for you. I want to enjoy every second."

She curled into my side and I held her naked body tightly against mine.

I found my Elysium.

We lay in naked repose quietly listening to each other's heart-beats. Her soft skin against mine is the only thing I want to feel for the rest of my life. After what I thought was only a few minutes, I stretched my free arm, checking my watch.

Holy shit...we were there for almost three hours.

"Charlie, we need to be getting back. It's after five," I whispered, stroking her face.

Feeling her muscles tighten and extend, a groan came from my shoulder, "Damn it. I fucking hate reality."

"Hey," I rolled to my side, "This *is* reality, Charlie. You and me...here."

I put my hand over her heart.

"I meant what I said. I love you and I'm not going anywhere. After we catch this guy...you and I will figure the rest out."

Her eyes gazed at me wide and round. I don't think I had ever told a woman I loved her. With my past, you would think that the mere idea of love and commitment would terrify me; but it didn't. At least, not with her. I would do anything, be anything she needed. I would jump in front of a moving train for her.

It was cliche, but no less true.

I pulled her against me once more, "Just five more minutes."

Charlie snuggled back into my side and I allowed my mind to drift. While recent images of her nude form floated through my head, and my body was starting to respond to them. I had to forcefully push them aside.

As I did, they slowly morphed and changed into a funnel of information with bits of knowledge beginning to waft from somewhere in my sub-conscience. I heard pieces of conversations from the FBI field office, from my past, and watched the pictures of the fires flipped like pages in my brain. More images floated to the surface. Knowledge, both past and present, congealed, transforming into puzzle pieces that were beginning to click into place.

"Son of a bitch!" I sat stick-straight in the bed.

Charlie gasped, "What's the matter?"

"Oh my God...I'm such an asshole, Charlie," I closed my eyes angrily.

In the dim light of the bedroom, I saw Charlie rise up, propping herself on an elbow.

"Yeah," she said, "it's part of your charm."

My eyes cut her like daggers.

"Okay...sorry...joking," she offered.

"I need to tell you something," I blurted hastily.

Charlie sat up on the bed, pulling a pillow out to cover her breasts. My brain ran in circles trying to figure out how I would say everything because this was going to be complicated and messy.

"What?" she asked curtly. "And remember, I have a gun."

The last comment I know was meant tongue-in-cheek, and as a joke, but I knew she would use it without question.

Closing my eyes again, I took a deep breath, "I think...damn it. I *know* who set the church fire...*all* the fires. And I think I know why."

Chapter Fifty-One

CHARLIE

My heart fell into my shaking legs; the orgasms he elicited from me hours earlier still had me weak. My heart raced and even though I sat nude except for the pillow covering me, I was able to bring Agent Hanson to the conversation.

"What do you mean you think you know?" I asked steadily.

Turning in the bed, Eric faced me, "You asked me the other day about the places that were destroyed in Vegas, remember?"

I nodded.

"I didn't recognize either location at the time, but I think I was wrong," Eric kept his voice steady. "The club? It was called Starlight when it torched...but five years ago, it was called Roxy. I went there... a lot."

"Okay," I nodded again. "How much is a lot?"

"A lot is first name basis with every waitress, bouncer, and bartender. Not to mention the owner," he swallowed hard, "I haven't placed the other fire...but the ones in Portland. The church? St. Lawrence? They held a St. Florian festival right after I moved there."

I shrugged.

"St. Florian is the patron saint of firefighters....it was really a community party where members of the public can get up close to equipment, rigs...meet the men and women of their local houses...stuff like that. "

I was starting to get it, and I was getting nervous that I had been right all along. Damn, Jack and Emile for questioning my gut. I wasn't the connection to these fires, Eric was.

I took a deep breath, "What about the house? What is your connection to that house?"

Eric shook his head, "Nothing. I've seen pictures of it prior to it burning...I've never set foot in that place before. I will say, it was a nice house. Corner lot. Good neighborhood...white picket fence—Shit. Shit, shit, shit!"

"What's wrong?" I watched him cautiously.

"Get dressed. We're leaving...now." He ordered, scrambling out of bed to find his castaway clothing.

I leaped from the bed and redressed in record time. I gathered the rest of my clothes, the real reason we were there, and met Eric back in my living room. His demeanor was rigid and irritable but I had to ask the obvious question. Eric said he knew who had set the fires and he knew why. So far, he only established what I suspected two days ago which was that he could be the link.

I put my hand on his chest, "Hey...first, you need to breathe. Why would someone do this to you?"

"Look...Charlie...I'm not the same guy as the one in high school. Hell, I'm not the same guy I was the night before the reunion. You have to believe that...I need you to believe that," he begged.

I heard the thunder outside my door and allowed it to pass before I opened my mouth to speak, "I understand. I don't give a damn about who you were...that's got nothing to do—"

Eric's eyes pleaded with me, "But it does! Don't you understand? Who I was has everything to do with this...I am so sorry that you got wrapped up in all of it. Nettie...Emile...the hotel...it's all *my* fault."

"Eric, I don't understand. Who? Who is doing this?" I pushed. For someone who excelled under pressure, he was starting to lose it and that scared me.

"I'll tell you on the way. We need to go, now."

Chapter Fifty-Two

ERIC

The rain fell in sheets and the darkened November sky glowed with city lights under the cloud-filled sky as I barreled south along the five highway toward Portland. Silent anticipation filled the truck's cab and I could feel the bubble was ready to burst. Charlie wasn't asking questions, which made me nervous. I needed her to get me started because I wasn't sure where to begin. The story I would tell seemed dramatic and over-the-top. More of a tale for a true-crime novel than real life.

I questioned how this *was* real life. How was it possible that this psychopathic nutbag was still after me?

After I felt like we had enough miles behind us, I glanced in Charlie's direction, "Ten years ago I met someone in a bar... the Roxy. We hit it off really, really fast, and before long, we were sleeping together."

She turned her body so that I had her full attention.

"It was only supposed to be a one-night stand, but it lasted a couple of weeks. I broke it off and that was that," I kept my eyes on the road. I was already ashamed and didn't think I could take Charlie's eyes judging me while I explained what a terrible person I was back then.

"Until...?" she pressed.

"I started getting hang-up phone calls at home and the station. At first, I didn't think anything of it and I certainly didn't think it was *her*. Then, I was finding dead animals on the landing of my apartment...things like mice and frogs. That got my attention," I grimaced.

"I bet."

"It didn't stop there. She started calling my captain with wild stories and when she didn't get the reaction she wanted from him, she moved up the chain to my battalion chief...I nearly lost my goddamn job," I barked.

"Over what? It couldn't be about her making some phone calls. What was she telling them?"

Charlie wasn't interrogating me; at least, it didn't feel that way. She looked genuinely concerned when I caught a glimpse of her face in the passing freeway lights.

"She gave my captain a sob story about her concern for me and my supposed drinking problem," my grip tightened on the steering wheel.

Charlie sighed, "You've told me—"

"No," My fingers tapping on the wheel. "She told him I was a falling down drunk and that I was drinking on the job! I had to piss in a cup every day for two weeks to prove she was a liar. But her lies got more elaborate and I became a wife-beater who killed our unborn child. It got so...insane. Luckily, after everything was done, I was able to convince the powers that be that she was the crazy one."

Her head tilted, "Eric, was she pregnant?"

"No! Absolutely not...I'm not stupid. If she was...that's a huge *if*...it sure as hell wasn't mine and I certainly didn't hit her or cause her to lose a child," I snapped, glaring at the road ahead.

Charlie raised her hands in defense, "I was just asking because...you know—"

Her voice trailed off.

"No...Charlie. That never happened back then," I softened my tone.

"What else? It must have been more than a few stories...so far, I'm not hearing much you could prove, and certainly nothing that meets a stalking charge," she urged.

"Well, she was relentless. I would show up for work or leave after a shift and she was there. I responded to calls and I would see her in the crowd...the phone calls, letters. I finally got enough for a judge to issue a restraining order," I explained.

"I'm guessing that wasn't enough," Charlie replied.

I shook my head, "No, it wasn't. But credit card fraud, impersonating a firefighter, and property damage will land a person in jail for a time. She cut the tires on my car, she spray-painted graffiti on the door of my apartment. Then, she stole my identity and took out seven credit cards in my name. The house, Charlie. She pretended to be me to take out a loan and put a down payment on a house on a corner lot, with a white picket fence. Sound familiar?"

I saw her mind thinking and it made me curious about what. Trying to keep my eyes on the road, I glanced in her direction when I could. I wanted her to say something, anything because the silence was unbearable. I wasn't sure if I conveyed exactly how crazy and how dangerous this woman was.

"How does a break up of a two-week-old relationship turn so fast? And how does that escalate to arson and murder?" Charlie's questions hung in the air between us.

Looking at her, I stated flatly, "She's crazy."

Charlie's face turned into, *'Yeah, no joke.'*

"No, I'm serious. When my restraining order came up for renewal after she did her time in county, she brought her psychiatrist with her as a character witness. He tried to tell the judge that she was cured of her obsession and was no longer a threat."

"Did the judge believe him?" she asked.

"No, she didn't. She's reissued the order every year since...until this year. I moved a thousand miles... I just never imagined she would follow," my voice trailed off. "Charlie, I'm so sorry. This is wholly my fault...Nettie is dead and Emile is in a coma because of me."

Shaking her head, Charlie paraphrased Gloria, "No, it's not. It's her fault...and we're going to get her."

Chapter Fifty-Three

CHARLIE

We rolled into the parking garage of headquarters around ten o'clock. The crime scene from Emile's shooting was already cleaned up except for the stain where he laid the night before. I winced as we walked over it and into the elevator. I never gave an emotional thought to what was left behind at a scene, but, then again, it never hit home like it did now.

Jack was sitting in the bullpen on the phone when we walked inside. His face spoke volumes and because we'd been partners for so long, I knew what he would say before he hung up the phone.

"Shit!" Jack slammed the receiver hard on the base. "Goddamn rookies. Who the hell told them to break off the search?"

"Jack," I soothed, "The rain's coming down in sheets and they've been looking for the driver since yesterday. We're not going to find her."

His face turned on me, "Her? You know the suspect is female?"

I never glanced at Eric. I didn't want him to suffer Jack's wrath if we were correct and Eric's stalker was behind all of this. I'd have to ease Jack into it. Turning on my computer, my fingers flew across the keyboard.

Keeping my voice low, I asked Eric, "Her name?"

"Marta Di Luca," he leaned over my shoulder and I smelled his cologne. My brain nearly disengaged from Agent Hanson and returned to being Charlie of the Quivering Thighs.

"Hello? How do you know our perp's a woman?" Jack called over from his desk. I refocused my eyes on the screen, shrugging my shoulders as if shaking my partner's boring eyes off me.

"Height, weight?" my fingers trailed over my keyboard. "In a minute Jack!"

I heard my partner mumble something about me making him wait. I'll admit, his grumbling makes me grin.

"Five foot nine...black hair, brown eyes."

After inputting all the details, I knew we would wait for a return of information. Turning to Eric, I discreetly put my hand over his, "Look, this may take a little while. I'll give you the key to my hotel room...why don't you go there and get some sleep?"

His mossy eyes stared at me.

I lowered my voice to a whisper, "I don't think you should stay at your house. We can be sure Marta already knows where you live. At least this way, you'll be safe. Oh...and take my rental."

I gave him my car keys and he continued his cocked eyebrow stare at me. "Humor me, okay?"

"Charlie...this is stupid. I'm a grown man...I don't need my..." he stopped and I smirked.

"Yes? Please continue," I urged, chuckling under my breath still trying to keep my partner out of earshot.

Eric leaned closer, his lips directly on my ear, "I don't need the woman I love more than life itself protecting me like a helpless child."

The cadence of his voice sent chills down my spine. I turned in my seat, looking up at him and his fierce, dark green eyes as we drilled into each other. He wanted me to stand down, but in light of recent events, that wasn't an option.

"Just take the keys. Go get a shower and come back here in a couple of hours," I offered.

Eric sighed, "Alright, two hours. Think you'll have a lead by then?"

"I'm going to get Jack to check on our search warrant," I turned back to my screen. "So, yeah...I think we'll definitely be ready."

"I'm going downstairs to grab coffee...our machine is broken here. You want anything?" Jack called from three cubicles over.

I looked around Eric's wide frame, "Yeah...bring me back a cup."

"Tilset?"

"Nah, I was just leaving," Eric's eyes never wavered from mine. He waited for a solid ten-count to make sure Jack was gone and squatted in front of me. "Hey—"

In this position, we were nearly face-to-face. Before I could answer, his lips were on me and his tongue was dancing slowly with mine. My knees shook.

Pulling away, he gave me one last sweet peck, "I love you."

He left me alone in the bullpen with a melting core and a racing heart.

Chapter Fifty-Four

ERIC

I wouldn't leave her ever again without her knowing how much I love her. That was an oath I made to myself after she let me make love to her today. She would never know loneliness or an absence of love ever again.

Jesus, I sound like a fucking Hallmark movie.

But, this is how I feel and nothing will change it. I felt lighter on my feet as I rode the elevator back to the parking garage. I really wanted to hop in my truck and take myself to my own shower, but if it made Charlie happy that I hid out a bit, then so be it. To my relief, I think she finally realized just how crazy Marta was and how far she would go to get what she wanted.

I clicked the remote to unlock Charlie's borrowed black Ford sedan when I felt something solid and round press into my lower spine.

"Move!" a woman's voice ordered. I began to turn around when she hissed, "Don't! Walk to your truck. You'll drive."

Walking to my truck, she led me to the passenger side. Opening the door, I slid over to behind the wheel while discreetly cutting my eyes in her direction. The black hood of her sweat-shirt was pulled low over her face and covered a dingy baseball cap. Her black jeans were wet and they and her boots were mud-caked. She held the handgun in her right hand using her left arm as a stand to steady the muzzle she pointed at an angle toward my temple.

"Drive through the gate...and if you alert the guard, I'll pull this trigger. So, unless you like the thought of your little girlfriend standing over your grave, you'll do what I say," she sneered.

I did as she asked and when we reached the road she ordered me to turn left. She spoke very little, but I noticed two things as she directed me through the city. One: we were quickly putting Portland in our rearview mirror and two: this woman wasn't Marta Di Luca.

Chapter Fifty-Five

ERIC

This highway was all too familiar for me. I spent my youth wandering along this two-lane stretch of road and every side path that branched from it. As the crow flies, we were less than ten miles from Hydrangea Falls. The woman in black ordered me to turn off onto a choppy field I knew very well.

I spent the entire drive out of the city wondering who the person holding the gun on me was. To my knowledge, I had no enemies to speak of, short of Marta, but this wasn't her, I was sure of it. This woman was too petite and held too much understanding of the area to be my stalking ex-girlfriend. I considered running us off the road, but with the wet road conditions, I didn't want to kill myself in the process of getting the upper hand.

When we came upon the cabin, I noticed the lights were on inside and there was a dark Indian motorcycle sitting under the lean-to on the far side of the edifice. I parked the truck just in front of the door, its headlights still shining on the front of the log building. I was surprised to see the red gingham curtains in the windows were still the same and the familiar porch swing was moving in the light breeze. My brain remembered the smell of the cedar floor before we ever walked inside.

I had been here a hundred times, or more, since birth. This was my grandparent's lake house.

My father's parents built this small two-room building as a fishing cabin for my grandfather, but my grandmother enjoyed it just as much as he did. As children, my brothers and I loved taking the short drive along the backroads to reach this place of quiet solitude that backed up to Bow Bend Lake. We would paddle the small canoe our grandparents owed, out to fish for trout and perch and the cool waters of the lake were great for swimming on hot summer days.

The cabin stayed in my family but now instead of closing it up for the winter, my parents made a bit of money off the rent they charged tenants in the off-season.

"Get out," the woman barked, leveling the gun at my head.

I did as she commanded, keeping my hands up in surrender as much as I could. I walked toward the door and she fell in step behind me. I knew I had to try and reason with her.

"The place looks good. I see you've taken care of it," I did my best not to sound threatening and remain calm.

"Shut up," she growled. "Open the door."

I recognized the familiar creaking of the metal hinges as it swung inside. When I stepped through, the muzzle of her gun shoved into my spine, I half expected to find an accomplice inside, but the room was empty except for some furniture and a pile of what looked like stuff from a garage sale.

"Pull out the chair and use the handcuffs to secure yourself," she shoved the gun into my back. I did as she said and took the two sets of handcuffs off the small kitchen table, locking one of the loops around the arms of the chairs then strapping myself in on the left side. She pointed the gun at my chest while locking my right wrist to the chair.

"You know, I might be having more fun if I knew who you were," if a trip down memory lane didn't work, I thought a joke might.

"Oh, sweetie. I'd love to take you up on that offer...but, we have some work to do first."

I could tell she was eyeing me under the covered brim of the dirty hat. I watched the whites of her eyes narrow.

She lowered her gun, "What the hell...I mean we only live once. That's why we're here after all."

Sitting the gun on the table she moved toward me slowly and straddled my lap. She put her lips to mine, planting a long, unpassionate kiss on them. I never kissed back but noticed that she wore lipgloss that had the flavor of strawberry sugar. It tasted cheap and something that a high school girl might use.

"How was that sweetie?" she smiled out of her hood. "Maybe we'll have some more of that later. But right now—"

She pulled on my shirt and the last two buttons flew off from the strain. She ran her hands over my chest, pulling my shirt over my shoulders to expose my torso. She began to grind against my hips and as she did, she removed her hooded sweatshirt and hat.

I sat in shock at the immediate recognition of the round face and brilliant blue eyes of the woman rocking on my lap.

Chapter Fifty-Six

CHARLIE

Three hours ticked by as I waited for an email that my history on Marta Di Luca was complete. Jack sat dozing in a nearby cubicle with his feet propped on the desk. I would be doing the same, but one of us had to work. It was then that I realized Eric was late returning from the hotel. With as much grief as he gave me about going, I assumed he'd be on time, if not early. I would give him a few more minutes...

"Charlie! Hey..." Jack shook my shoulder.

I sat up and my back made horrible cracking sounds as I did. I looked at my phone to see how long I had been out.

An hour and a half.

"Where's Eric?" I yawned.

Jack handed me another cup of coffee, "I was about to ask you the same question."

I choked.

"What do you mean? He hasn't come back?" I nearly threw myself out of the chair, spilling coffee down my dark jeans.

"No. If he's smart, he's at home asleep," my partner took a pull from his cup, handing me a Kleenex. I stared at him for a moment. I knew Eric wasn't sleeping and I was sure he wasn't at home. But where did he go?

Grabbing my coat, I barreled past Jack, "C'mon!"

"Where are we going?" he called after me, entering the wide hallway where the bank of elevators lived. Jack jogged after me as I pushed through the fire door to the stairwell.

I was already a flight down before he caught up.

"Hey...Charlie...what's going on?" he panted as he ran after me.

I picked up my quick pace, "He was supposed to come back two hours ago."

When we reached the basement's steel door, I bulldozed it with my shoulder and it made a small clanging sound against the concrete pillar. The garage was all but bare with a few of the cars parked belonging to agents, cleaning crews, and security personnel still in the building. Nothing seemed out of place in the nearly empty lot except that my car was still there and Eric's truck was gone.

"Damn it!" my teeth ground and I stood looking at the cameras in the nooks of the parking garage's corners. Jack's eyes followed mine.

"Charlie...out with it. I see the wheels turning..." he remarked.

Facing him, I let out a long breath, "We might have a lead on who the arsonist is...Marta Di Luca, of Las Vegas, Nevada."

"Who is she?" Jack's brown eyes watched me closely.

"Ex-flame. One of those he-broke-it-off-and-she-didn't kinda situations," turning away from my partner, I marched to the elevator. I felt his eyes again staring into the back of my head.

"Uh huh...what are we talking here? Some drunk desperate phone calls or Fatal Attraction?" he slid into the lift next to me.

"The latter, from the sound of it...I've got her sheet on the computer. Guess I dozed off before I could get a good look at it. Anyway...I gave Eric the keys to my ride and told him to go to the hotel and shower. He was supposed to be back hours ago. My car is here, he's gone," I cut my eyes in Jack's direction.

He nodded, "I'll get Rolando in tech to get me the video of the parking garage...I want to see her history."

Jack was on the phone as we walked into the task force command center's bullpen once more. I went to work printing off a copy of Marta's criminal history when I noticed something odd. The document listed her birthday, birth name, aliases, and charges going back ten years. When my eyes fell to the bottom of the last page, my stomach dropped into my feet. It was the same feeling I got on roller coasters. My heart raced so fast I thought I might vomit.

"Jack," I called out across the room. Still, on the phone, my partner crossed the space to peer over my shoulder.

"Lando, I need that video *now*... We might have a problem," Jack hung up his cell phone. He continued to stare at the page for what seemed like several minutes.

Thoughts tore through my brain faster than I could catch them. The proof that Marta Di Luca was innocent stared back at my partner and me; cold, impartial, and objective. I couldn't argue and even if I could, I didn't have words.

Marta Di Luca was dead.

CHAPTER FIFTY-SEVEN

CHARLIE

"Marta Angeline Di Luca died of an apparent self-inflicted gunshot wound on June 7 in her home. The Clark County coroner has released the body to relatives and has no additional comment," sitting at my desk, I read the story aloud to Jack. "Shit!"

I pushed away from my desk. I looked out of the row of windows and watched the sun barely peeking over the horizon. Closing my eyes, I dug the heels of my palms into them and imagined what my next move would be. I reevaluated. If Marta was dead and had been dead for months, there was no way she was responsible for what was happening since her death. Could she have still started the fire that killed Nettie? It was a possibility, but not probable. My gut pulled me in a direction that I couldn't yet see. There was still someone hiding in the shadows, beyond the smoke and mirrors just barely out of reach.

"What are you talking about?" Jack's voice was rising in volume. "I don't have those fucking reports. Yeah...that would be swell. No...I need them now!"

He slammed the phone on his desk back on the receiver.

"What's wrong?" I opened my eyes.

Jack's face was ruddy and he looked as though he may explode at any moment, "The goddamn lab has results back from the fires...but they've forgotten to send the reports."

He glared, "They've been *busy*."

The sardonic sound of my laughter left my chest before I could control it, "Oh, and we haven't? Jesus Christ...we need those results. Any way we can get one of them on the phone when they come in?"

"Consider it done," Jack reached for his receiver.

While my partner kicked over a beehive, I called Eric but got no answer. I was beginning to worry about his whereabouts and the worry made me feel weird. It had been a lot of years since I had been in a relationship and I didn't want to jump in too far.

But, then again, even friends get concerned about one another, right?

Deciding I needed to hear something good, I called Gloria to check on Emile. Her expressive and lilting voice was the music my ears needed at five in the morning. The hospital began an hour prior reducing the medication keeping Emile in a coma. It seemed they were seeing positive signs that his brain swelling was decreasing and they were confident he would make a full recovery. After promising I would come by later that day, I placed the receiver back on its cradle and called Eric's phone once more.

Still no answer.

I stood from my desk and stretched. Jack slapped me on the back, "Let's go Hanson. The lab is on Zoom."

Chapter Fifty-Eight

CHARLIE

"Hanson...Brent. You two look like shit," Micheal Bristow, the lab supervisor in Quantico and all-around dickhead chortled. "Hippies in Oregon don't have showers for you to use?"

I was in no mood for his douchebaggery, "Look, Mike...if your techs had sent the results days ago, maybe we could have caught this guy and would be back home right now instead of camping out in this office that's starting to smell like Jack's shitter after he eats Taco Bell. So, either tell us what you've got or get off the line so I can have some decent fucking coffee delivered."

His giant head stared at me through the wide-screen television.

He raised his eyebrows, "Okay...sharing my screen now..."

Jack cut his eyes at me and I could see he was holding back tears of laughter. It was the same reaction he had every time I lost my patience with anyone, especially certain co-workers who got on his nerves as well.

"Most of what ignited the fires was nearly completely consumed with the pentane," Mike's screen filtered pictures of the fires, lining them against corresponding test results. "Which, as a side note, is a crazy accelerant to choose."

"Crazy, how?" Jack chewed on the end of a Bic pen.

"I just mean, out of a dozen hydrocarbons, pentane isn't exactly the most common. You'd have to be familiar with it," he shrugged on screen.

"What else?" I pushed, wanting to get to the meat of the findings.

"Well, we were able to identify a few articles of clothing and odd remnants of paper from three of the fires." We watched Mike move his cursor to a picture of the St. Lawrence fire, bringing it to the front. "We tested what we believed to be a dress used to start this fire. The dress was a polyester blend...pretty common...color name is Magenta FF zero zero nine zero."

"Which is what, exactly?" Jack snickered. "A recipe?"

"It's bright pink. Keep going Mike," Rolling my eyes I continued to prod the conversation along.

The lab tech cleared his throat, "Next up, we've got what looks to be a school-type shirt used at the condo fire in Seattle. We've been able to pull some sort of mascot from the shirt using some fancy reverse photography techniques."

Mike's cursor hovered over an image of a darkened negative photograph that clearly showed the head of a Wildcat. I felt the arteries in my temples pulse and I fought against the urge to vomit again. I recognized the image because I myself *owned* that same shirt at one time.

"It looks like a—" Mike explained until I cut him off.

"Wildcat." My throat was a desert and the room went silent. From my peripheral, I saw Jack's entire body turn in my direction, but I was frozen and confused. My mind galloped in a hundred different directions trying to put together a puzzle that was still missing its pieces.

Without looking away, Jack continued, "What's the last thing, Mike?"

"Uh...yeah. Well, this was a little tougher. This is from the Hydrangea Falls fire...the perp used what we think was a paper product...like toilet paper or napkins, which, as you can imagine, burn very thoroughly. There was also latex residue melted next to the incendiary...balloons of some sort. It was a mess to go through since that building was a total loss," Mike flipped through pages of a paper file.

Balloons? Those weren't normal decor for my aunt's church.

"What's the significance of the balloons?" I finally swallowed back the growing lump in my throat.

Mike frowned, shrugging his shoulders, "I'm not that kind of agent, Charlie. That's kinda *your* job."

"Were balloons found anywhere else in the building? Were they only found as part of or near the origin? Could you determine a color?" I shot questions like bullets.

His condescension wore me thin.

I kept one eye on my phone, watching the time. Eric still hadn't called or returned and the more time this idiot spoke, the more rattled I became.

"No. No other balloons were found and those were only near the origin of the fire. The techs weren't able to pull a color per se...but did get metallic flaring from the evidence."

Mike's tone told me he was as done with me as I was with him. Jack scribbled the last of his notes on his pad.

"Okay, Mike. Thanks...we'll call back if we need anything," he disconnected the video feed before the man could respond. Jack turned to face me. "What the fuck was that?"

I shook my head. I was doing my damnest to pull what Mike just told us into focus.

"Oh, hell no, Charlie...you look like you saw a ghost. I see your brain working...what's your gut saying?" Jack pushed.

Goddamn it. My gut and my brain were on two very different levels. The image of the Wildcat symbol had me a little spooked. It was clear this was personal, and up until now, my intuition told me it was tied to Eric, but we attended the same high school. My clear path just became obstructed again.

"Jack, I'm not sure...at least, not anymore."

He pointed a finger at me, "You keep thinking, I'm getting Dana on the horn. She's had enough time to analyze the guest list from the search warrant. We need to cross-reference everyone on that list to Eric *and* you."

He left the conference room, heading for his desk. I knew my brain wasn't firing on all cylinders. I didn't know what I needed worse; coffee, or three days of uninterrupted sleep. Rays of light poured into the windows as dawn fully broke. My head throbbed and I rubbed at my temples. Feeling the table vibrate, I looked over to see Jack's cell phone next to me. The name read *Sparky*.

Carrying the phone to Jack's desk, I mouthed, "Phone?"

"Answer it," he whispered, covering the mouthpiece of the receiver.

I drew the green icon to the right, "Jack Brent's phone."

A familiar voice on the other line paused and then answered, "Hey Dick."

CHAPTER FIFTY-NINE

CHARLIE

E^{ric?}

My brain was on fire. Why was he calling Jack? Why didn't he answer any of my calls?

Why was he calling Jack by another name?

I played along, "Yeah...it's Dick."

"Hey...I won't be in for the rest of the week. I had some family stuff come up...I've had to go home for a few days," he stated flatly, but I detected a bit of relief when I chose to join the charade.

I grabbed a pen and wrote Eric's name on Jack's notebook, shoving it in my partner's face. He immediately told Dana he could call her back. Cell phones weren't the best devices for quiet conversations so I lowered the pitch of my voice as best I could.

"What number can I reach you at? Still your cell?" I did my best to mimic a masculine tone.

I almost heard a smile in his voice, "Yeah...I'll have to bring you fishing sometime. Lots of Greenling, Perch, and Sunfish...look, I got to go."

"Eric?" my voice was now husky with fear.

The line was dead.

My hands shook with anger, "Someone has him."

"Charlie...listen to me. We'll get him back...did he give you any clues?"

I took a deep breath. I had to center myself and let my emotions go. I refused to allow anything to cloud my judgment because it was clear that it could cost Eric his life.

"Yeah. Okay...he said he had family stuff...he had to go home. He's in the Falls," I nodded.

Jack wrote frantically, "What else?"

"I asked about his phone...he said he'd take me fishing. Greenling, Perch, and Sunfish..." I continued to murmur the names of the fish because they didn't sound right in my mouth. "Greenling...Perch...Sunfish."

"What's the matter?" Jack's eyes narrow on me.

"It doesn't sound right...I've never fished for Greenling at home—" The enormous smile spread across my mouth, "Oh...Tilset. Smart man...smart, smart man."

"What?"

"Jack! You don't fish for Greenling anywhere near Hydrangea Falls...it's hard to find a saltwater fish in *fresh* waters," a temporary relief washed over as pieces started to fall into place. "Get HRT on the phone...I think I know where he is!"

Within fifteen minutes the deserted task force room was filled with agents being apprised of the possible ongoing hostage situation. As Jack and I ran down the details of the past hour, no less than twenty times, all in an effort to get our teams on the road quickly, the bureau's Hostage Response Team, or HRT assembled downstairs.

Details of the last six hours were also coming into focus. The videotape of the garage showed a shorter person in black jeans and a hoodie brandishing a weapon and leading Eric to his truck. The perp knew they were being watched, keeping their baseball cap low over their eyes, and never looking toward any camera.

An hour after Eric's call to Jack, we were leaving Portland and headed straight for my hometown.

"Charlie," Jack tapped my shoulder as he sat behind me in the armored SUV, "you're sure this person isn't also holding his parents?"

I shook my head sharply, watching the skyline of Portland becoming smaller in the sideview mirror, "No. I've spoken to his mother...they're safe at their farm. The local LEO's have someone watching their place. The only location Eric could be is his grandparent's cabin. It's great for Perch and Sunfish."

The names of the fish were still rolling through my head. Why would Eric specifically pick those species? Two freshwater and one salt. No, it was one salt and two fresh. That order had to be important.

GPS.

"Jack!" I exclaimed, turning around sharply in my seat. "Get tactical on the radio...they need to ping Eric's cell phone...his GPS locator is active!"

He stared at me momentarily, "Greenling, Perch, Sunfish. Oh...good job my man."

It took Dana five minutes to get a lock on the phone; we had confirmation that Eric and his captor were at the cabin at Bow Bend Lake and we would be there within the hour. Not wanting to waste a second, I turned back to Jack.

"We get that data from the search warrant yet?"

Jack pulled two, identical file folders out of his go bag, handing me one, "Here...run through these names and see if you recognize anyone."

The file contained pages of names of guests who checked into the Doubletree within a week of my arrival in Portland and in the week prior to the two fires there. The lists of names from the time of the blazes gave me nothing but as I turned to the second set of names from the past week, someone caught my eye. It took me several minutes to process what I was reading much in the same way it startles the mind when you see a co-worker at the grocery store.

But it was there in black and white. Immediately, my conversation with the lab supervisor, Mike, became crystal clear. The balloons. The Wildcat. The pink dress. The short, nearly shapeless figure in black with the gun pointed at Eric's back.

She used her married name, but it didn't change the fact that the person we were after was my former friend, Audrey Campbell.

Chapter Sixty

ERIC

Her blue eyes sparkled as she tittered around the tiny kitchen tidying up the few dishes in the sink and wiping counters. I watched every move she made hoping she would, at some point, either put the gun down or put it within my reach. Not that I could go anywhere really, she had me tied to this chair.

With her back turned, I placed some gentle, but firm pressure on the handcuffs. I certainly didn't think I could break the steel shackles, but I knew this chair was old and maybe I could split the wood. I also wanted to get some damn answers.

"Audrey...this plan doesn't seem very well put together. Not like your others," I kept my tone level while the metal of the cuffs cut into my wrists.

She moved over to the small apartment-sized gas range and began softly wiping its white enamel finish, "What do you mean?"

"I mean," I took a quiet breath before fighting against my restraints again, "Those were planned...well executed. You put a gun to my back and kidnapped me from FBI Headquarters. Not very smart."

She immediately turned on me, her face twisting with fury, "I am *very* smart! You and the princess with the badge had no idea, did you? How could you? I'm that good!"

She pointed a well-manicured nail in my face.

"So this is about Charlie?" I clarified and Audrey rolled her eyes.

"Humph. Precious little Charlie. Jesus...if they only knew about her...what a self-righteous...selfish..." she was muttering and returned to cleaning. I let her talk to herself for a couple of minutes just to hear what she was thinking.

It didn't help.

"Audrey?" I said softly. She turned back to me, abandoning her task to sit on my lap.

"Mmmmm?" she purred. "What can I do for you, Mr. Tilset? I'm sure we can think of something...*fun*...to do to pass the time."

She licked my ear and I instinctually moved away from her. My involuntary action immediately evoked hate-filled anger and she bit my lobe, hard. I winced, feeling a small trickle of what I was sure was blood sliding down my neck.

"Behave yourself, naughty boy. Or I might have to do something you'll regret," she whispered the threat in my ear, but its meaning rang loud. She pulled back, looking me in the eyes with a sly grin, "You'd like that though, huh? You're like me...you like a little danger. A little adventure? Maybe I'll invite Charlie to watch us. She can sit here while you drive your cock into me like you did to her the other night. Whatdya think?"

She raised an eyebrow, staring at me.

I have never felt the need to be violent toward any woman, not even Marta. Have I been a philandering asshole? Yes, but I have never laid a hand on any woman in any way she didn't want or like.

I wanted to shove Audrey Campbell through the wall.

"Get off me," I ordered.

"Oh...I'll get off on you soon enough," she stroked a finger down my jaw. "You'll see things my way...and when you do, you'll see I'm the better choice. You'll forget all about my dearest, washed-up harlot."

I was getting angrier by the second. I had to get out of these cuffs, but the only way was to play her game. I was out of options.

I returned her hardened stare, "Convince me."

Audrey paused. "What?"

"Convince me I should choose you," I nosed her face and positioned my lips dangerously close to hers. It elicited the reaction I wanted. Audrey's wide smile spread across her face as her eyes rolled seductively.

She ran her fingernail down my chest, "How?"

"You're a smart woman, I'm sure you could think of something," I dropped my voice in her ear. She repositioned herself to straddle my lap and she started grinding against me. My hatred and contempt for this woman filled me and I used it to fight off any natural responses my body would have. There was no way I would give her that satisfaction, but I still had to lead her where I wanted her to go.

Writhing in fake discomfort, I groaned painfully, "Baby...you got to stop. I'm not in the right position for that."

She immediately stopped moving.

"I'm so sorry," her eyes begged for approval.

"It's okay...we don't need to move so fast. Just sit here and keep me company," I forced a smile. I nuzzled her face once more, moving closer to her mouth. Without hesitation, her lips latched on and she shoved her tongue down my throat.

Her kiss was quick and manic. She lapped at my mouth like a dog desperate for a drink of water. It was certainly not the sweet perfection that Charlie's mouth produced.

Our kiss broke and I unwillingly smiled at her, "See? That's nice."

Her lips found every inch of my neck before returning to my mouth. We made out like inadequate junior high kids for what had to have been a half hour before she spoke again and I braved to move on with my plan.

"Are you convinced yet?" her hands entwined behind my neck and played with the back of my nearly shaven head.

I gave her a slight grin, "Almost."

"What else can I do to satisfy your loyalty?" she removed her sweatshirt to reveal a tight-fitting tank top that hugged all of her curves.

If she wasn't a murdering psycho, I would have said she was quite pretty.

She climbed closer to my torso, placing her heaving breasts at face level. She pressed her fleshy mounds into my chin and I looked down into her deep cleavage.

"I'd say we're getting warmer," I forced another smile. "Unlock one of these handcuffs."

Her eyes narrowed on me.

"I want to be able to touch you," I offered quickly. Reaching into her jeans, she produced the small key and unlocked my right hand. Not wanting to lose ground, I promptly wrapped my free hand around her head, pulled her close, and kissed her. Her body relaxed.

I stared deep into her eyes, "Show me more, and tell me why you hate Charlie."

Her bizarre giggle of delight sent chills down my spine.

CHAPTER SIXTY-ONE

CHARLIE

"What's our ETA?" Jack barked into his headset. We were gearing up on the road and would take the lead just as HRT hit the ground at the cabin.

A man's voice crackled in the earpiece, "Ten minutes."

I felt the Suburban lurch as our driver, a younger rookie agent with piercing blue eyes, pressed the gas pedal harder. Jack passed my bullet-proof vest to me and I slid the unit over my head.

"What's the background with you and this woman?" Jack's voice muffled as he pulled on his vest.

I chuckled, "How far back do you want me to go?"

"Well," he grunted as he strapped the thick Velcro bindings, "give me what you got."

I wasn't sure where to begin. Audrey Campbell and I grew up together since our first day of kindergarten. There was a point in our lives when the pair of us were inseparable. Sleepovers, birthday parties, and even in Sunday school you could find me and Audrey giggling about something. But, life moves on, kids change, and we'd found our paths diverging. It was the natural and normal evolution of growing up.

"I mean, we were close friends as children...until some time in high school. I mean, we weren't *not* friends...our interests just didn't meet up. She was a cheerleader...student council, stuff like that. I was more of an academic...did some choir," I shrugged.

Jack sniggered, "You can sing?"

"Shut up."

"Have any of the same friends?" Jack continued, still laughing under his breath.

"Well, yeah...there were only about a hundred people in our class. We knew everyone," I checked the time on my phone. I knew we would be arriving at the dirt road leading to the cabin any second. We would set an outer perimeter before breaching the inner quadrant of the property.

"That's not what I asked...did you have the same friends?"

"Yeah, I guess. We pretty much hung out with the same people. If you're asking if we were besties, the short answer is no...you know how it is in high school. Besides, that was so long ago. You can't think she held onto some stupid grudge for this long," I dismissed the idea. "Besides, if either of us should have a right to one it would be me."

I knew my partner and could almost hear his brow raise at the back of my head, "Why is that Hanson?"

Turning in my seat, I sighed, begrudgingly giving him an explanation, "She slept with my husband. Which is why he's my ex-husband."

I expected chortles, shock, and a little ribbing from him. But, I got none of it. What I did see in his eyes was empathy. Jack understood all too well how having a cheating spouse hurts, no matter how bad the relationship was or how wrong you were for each other.

He nodded in understanding, "That's not something that's easy to forgive."

"Honestly, Jack, it's been so long ago it doesn't matter. And she probably saved me from more heartache and headaches in the long run. I should probably buy her dinner actually. Anyway, I saw Audrey and her husband at the reunion six months ago, everything seemed fine." I felt the SUV slow to a near crawl before turning onto the narrow country road.

We had arrived.

Chapter Sixty-Two

ERIC

"Hate Charlie?" she smiled deviously. "You have it all wrong...I don't hate her. Am I angry with her? Yes...but she should know better. You can't be best friends with someone one day and the next turn your back on them. It's not right. You can't go back on a promise."

Caressing her shoulder, I nodded as though I understood, "She did that to you?"

"You didn't know? Don't you remember, we were nearly attached at the hip as kids. Our moms even called us *twins*...as a joke, of course," she kissed my lips in short pecks.

I cleared my throat, always keeping my free hand moving softly across her skin, "Is that why you burned down the church? To teach her a lesson?"

She pulled away, searching my face. She was looking for any indication that I was lying or leading her on, which I was. I took her face in my hand, stroking her cheek, offering the minute act of comfort.

Audrey pressed her head into my hand, closing her eyes, "I was just so...angry with her. All these years she couldn't take five minutes to ask me how I was. It was like being in high school all over again...and she promised we would share everything."

"What about Nettie? You surely didn't mean to hurt her," I leaned my forehead on hers.

"I don't want to talk about this anymore," she began pulling at the button on her jeans. "You said you wanted me to take more off, right?"

I swallowed hard. I just had to keep the ruse up a little bit longer until Charlie found me. Surely she'd deciphered my code by now, I mean, it's not like it was really difficult to figure out. I was going to be pissed if I had to fuck this crazy woman.

"Slowly...please," I licked my lips for her satisfaction. It worked because she moaned delightfully.

"Oh, you are a naughty boy."

"Why did you come to Vegas?" I squeezed her ass cheek and she moaned again.

"I wanted to see you," she groaned.

"Why didn't you? I would have liked to see you," I traced the outline of her soft breast with my open hand.

"Well," her breath was shallow, "I know that now...but, you looked so sad. I thought you were missing *her*. That made me so angry...I didn't want you to be pining over her. Then, I met Marta. You know, she followed you around like a lost puppy...poor woman. She told me all about your relationship...I knew she wasn't right in the head, you know? I just wanted to help...I knew she was dragging you down too. That's why I tried to erase all your memories of Marta...just to help. It was the least I could do after the way Charlie treated you. Then I knew...Charlie had to learn *her* lesson. You can't treat people like that."

My heart was pounding as I realized that there was someone far more dangerous than Marta. I didn't know if I could wait for the calvary; I had to put some serious distance between myself and this cabin.

Just as I devised my plan, as inelegant as it was, a sound louder than thunder shook the old cabin. In the split second that it took Audrey to scream, I shoved her as hard as I could into the small kitchen table. Picking up the chair still handcuffed to my left wrist, I threw it against the wall and the old wood shattered into pieces. I slipped the crossbar I was shackled to out of the cuff and turned for the door.

What I saw in the small living area stopped me in my tracks. In the middle of the room, Audrey built a small pyre of keepsakes. Next to the pile of clothing, pompoms, and yearbooks was a canister labeled Pentane- Highly Flammable.

Reaching for the door, I heard the furious woman scream behind me as she scrambled from the floor. I swung the door wide when something caught my foot, tripping me on the beaten wood porch. I looked up to see men in tactical gear pointing rifles in my direction.

"Eric!" Charlie's voice called out from somewhere in the yard.

I scrambled to my feet when I felt the familiar feel of steel digging into my spine.

Chapter Sixty-Three

CHARLIE

I heard Audrey yell at Eric not to move. I looked at Jack and he was already shaking his head.

"Charlie...don't," he warned. "Let the negotiator handle it."

"I can talk to her, Jack. I'll reason with her," I argued, rising from behind the large armored tactical unit. Walking around its corner, I held my hands in the air, my gun securely in the waistband of my pants. "Audrey? It's Charlie...let's talk okay? You don't need to hurt anyone else."

"Goddamn it! Charlie!" Jack barked. "Charlie!

I ignored him. Fanned on either side of me, stood three HRT elite officers holding HK416 assault rifles fixed on Audrey. I walked between the two teams, easing my way closer to the porch. As much pain as she had caused, I didn't want them to kill her.

"Audrey...listen to me, let Eric go. You and I can talk...I don't want these good people to shoot you. Audrey, are you listening?" I called to my former friend.

"Charlie, what are you doing?" Jack's voice cracked in my ear.

Moving my wrist closer to my face, I spoke into the microphone, "Jack...we need to know why. She's already hurt too many people. We can take her alive."

"Keep the line open," he hissed.

"Roger."

I left the mic hot so Jack and everyone in the truck could hear my conversation. Taking another step, I watched Eric shake his head and his shoulder shove forward.

"That's close enough, Charlie!" he called out.

I immediately stopped.

"Eric, are you okay?"

"She says this is all your fault," he paused. "You shouldn't have abandoned her. You promised you'd always be friends...you're a liar."

I noticed the cadence of his voice was off and it took me a minute to realize she was talking through him.

"Audrey...you need to talk to *me*," I stepped closer. "Please, explain how I abandoned you...I want to understand."

I was two yards from the first riser of the tiny, wood portico.

"Charlie...don't!" This time Eric spoke for himself, "She's ready to blow this place."

Jack broke in, "Find out if it's the same setup as the other fires."

I nodded at Eric.

"All she wanted was your attention...for you to notice. Then you moved away and she never saw you. It was hurtful." He was speaking for her again. "You broke your promise."

It was a little unbelievable to me that she would hold a grudge for some nonexistent slight for twenty years. I quickly realized that I wouldn't be able to reason with her because she was delusional, but I had to try. As much as I hated her right now, I didn't want her dead and I knew if HRT had a shot, they would take it. "Audrey. I had to leave...you slept with my husband."

The best I could do was hit her with facts.

"No I didn't!" she screamed.

I put my foot on the step, "You did, Audrey. I came home that night and you were naked on my couch."

"No! No, I wasn't...I didn't do that. I wouldn't do that to you. He...must have forced me..."

I wasn't unfamiliar with assault accusations, and I always took the side of the victim. But, in Audrey's case, I knew this wasn't true.

"Audrey, you know that's not what happened. Davy is a lot of things. A thief and an addict, yes...but he's not a rapist. You and he were having an affair long before I caught you," I pulled myself onto the porch and could almost reach out and touch Eric. It was then I saw a sapphire eye peeking through a crack in the door. Audrey held the gun pointed up toward the base of Eric's skull but was careful to keep the door between her body and the outside.

Not that some old wood could stop the trained snipers in the yard.

"Don't come any closer or I'll pull this trigger," she warned sternly.

"Audrey...let him go. Eric has nothing to do with this...it's me you want. Let him go, we'll go inside and talk," I held out my hand in an offering.

"Hanson! What the fuck are you doing?" Jack yelled in my ear.

"Charlie...no. I'm not leaving you," Eric ground his jaw.

Keeping my voice even, I urged Audrey to take my offer, "Please...let him go. Just you and I...we can talk all of this out."

I watched the barrel of the gun move to point at my chest. Through the small opening, I saw her nod her head.

"Eric, get out of here. Now." I ordered, never removing my eyes from hers.

"No," he growled.

"Don't argue," I moved my index finger just out of Audrey's eyeline, pointing at my ear. "Trust me."

I watched Eric considering all of his options, but I was only giving him one. I needed him to get out of the way and out of danger. I wouldn't risk him getting hurt. The muscles in his jaw flexed as he slowly stepped off onto the lawn before being whisked away by an agent.

My eyes never moved off Audrey's position, "Okay... it's just us. Thank you for letting him go...there's no need for anyone to get hurt."

She laughed, "Except for me right? But, it's second nature for you to hurt me right?"

"Audrey, I don't know what you think I did to hurt you...but I am sorry you feel that way." She may not believe me, but I was very earnest.

Her laughter built into wet sobs, "You've done nothing your whole life but hurt me! I tried...I tried so hard to be your friend...but you didn't want anything to do with me. I tried so hard. It wasn't fair. Then...then you left and I thought you would call or write. But I had to hear about your life from your aunt. You never came home...never. Then I saw you at the reunion...and I thought it was finally my chance for us to be together again...but you blew me off. You didn't have time for me. But, you know what I realized? You're just a bitch to every-one...that's when I decided...you're promises mean nothing! I had to stop you."

"Audrey...we were friends a long time ago. People grow...they change. I've lived a lot of life since leaving the Falls. Let me help you now...let me show you how much I care," taking a small step to the right, I moved to get a better look into the cabin, her eyes, and gun following me. I saw a glimpse of a large silver canister. "Audrey, let's talk about the fires...why pentane?"

Her tears stopped, "I got it from a lab...it was easy."

"Audrey...come out of the cabin," I watched her eye disappear from the small opening. "Audrey?"

"Charlie...what's going on?" Jack snapped in my earpiece.

I immediately drew my weapon, shaking my head, "I don't know...I've lost visual. I'm going in."

I pushed the door open with my palm, my Sig leveled at whatever was lying beyond it. I sidestepped through the door just as Audrey dumped the contents of the canister onto the floor. The smell hit me like a wall as I was overcome with the fumes.

"Audrey! No! Don't do it!" My eyes watered.

"Hanson! Report!" Jack barked.

"Target escalation...tell teams to be aware of flammable liquid contamination," I kept my weapon trained on my former friend. "Audrey...what are you doing?"

She stepped into the center of a pile of clothing and books, "I tried, Charlie. I tried for so long to get your attention...for you to notice me. You finally did."

Audrey pulled a lighter out of the pocket of her jeans, holding it up so I could see it. Her eyes were drowning in gigantic tears but as she held her lighter steady, the hand holding the snub-nosed revolver shook. I knew she was terrified to pull the trigger, but she would most definitely light this place up. Fire was her friend.

"Yeah, I did notice, Audrey. But, I wonder why I had to...what is it about *me*, Audrey? I don't understand...you slept with my husband...ruined my marriage...and somehow, our estrangement is my fault? It doesn't make sense," I reasoned.

She lowered her gun, "You weren't supposed to leave... you were supposed to see him for what he was. A cheater...a ruiner! You were supposed to thank me! You were perfect until he got his hooks in you."

"How?" I asked steadily as she started mumbling to herself. I knew she was beginning to unravel. "Audrey, listen to me...how was Davy a ruiner?"

Still, with her gun at her side, she waved the unstruck lighter at me, "He took you...your purity...your...your..." She screamed in frustration, "We made a promise together! You were supposed to be my Dearest!"

"Listen to me, Audrey. I'm here now...I need you to put the gun and the lighter down. I know you don't want to hurt me or yourself," I attempted to calm the woman ever spiraling out of control.

She laughed wildly through tears and snot, "That's where you're wrong."

The next few moments felt like walking through quicksand while the world and my reflexes took over.

Chapter Sixty-Four

ERIC

"This way, sir!" It was a man's voice that barked orders from behind the helmet and goggles. Flipping his rifle behind him, he grabbed onto my arm as another person took his place on the line. He guided me around the sleek, black van I was sure was the command center. "Do you need medical attention?"

I saw him eyeing my bitten earlobe.

"No, I'm fine," I tried to look back at Charlie, but the man continued pulling me until we were fully behind the massive rig.

"I've got him," Jack Brent nodded at my escort. "Tilset...I need to know what's going on in that cabin."

Stepping into the enormous apparatus, I saw four agents wearing headsets, sitting at small workstations, and watching video screens of everything going on outside. I nodded to Jack, "That cabin is around five hundred square feet, open floor plan."

"That we know," he interrupted. "I need to know what incendiary device the perp has."

I could hear Charlie's voice.

"You're listening? Turn it up," I pointed to a speaker embedded in the control panel.

Jack obliged, "Tilset!"

"She's got a pile of what looks like crap from her attic...yearbooks, clothes...and enough fuel to take down half of downtown Hydrangea Falls," I was trying to listen to the conversation as I spoke. We heard Audrey crying. "Jack, listen to me...you've got to get Charlie out of there. Audrey is obsessed with her. It's almost like...a rejected love interest. I don't think she handled Charlie moving on and having her own life."

"That's becoming more obvious," he snapped.

I shoved his shoulder, "Goddamn it! Get her out of there...Audrey is going to kill Charlie and herself!"

"Audrey...come out of the cabin...Audrey?"

"Charlie! What's going on?" Jack snapped angrily, looking at me. "Look, Tilset...you've got to trust her...and me."

"I don't trust the crazy bitch in that cabin, Jack!" I bellowed as I felt four sets of eyes turn on us.

"I don't know...I've lost visual. I'm going in." Charlie's radio crackled as seconds moved like Christmas honey.

"Audrey! No! Don't do it!"

Jack yelled into the room, "Hanson! Report!"

"Target escalation...tell teams to be aware of flammable liquid contamination."

I heard Charlie cough over the speaker and knew the fumes had to be overwhelming in the confined space of the cabin.

There was nothing I could do but listen in near panic as the next few moments played out. I was a fireman, not a cop.

"Audrey! Put it down! Down! Now Audrey!"

I wanted to run back into that cabin and yank Charlie out of there, but I'm smart enough to understand that would never happen. I wouldn't make it beyond this truck before being tackled by the federal government's finest. I was helpless. I suddenly understood why Charlie's other relationships failed. This. This moment. Fear that I would never hold her again and anger at the person who put her in the situation rendered me impotent and paralyzed me.

I was furious. But I stood shoulder to shoulder with Jack, listening like childish spies to the conversation taking place twenty-five yards beyond where we stood.

"Listen to me, Audrey. I'm here now...I need you to put the gun and the lighter down. I know you don't want to hurt me or yourself."

Audrey's insane laughter bellowed from the speakers seconds before a final warning and gunfire rang over the air.

CHAPTER SIXTY-FIVE

ERIC

I flew out of the mobile task force unit, my feet never touching the step as I tore across the front yard of the tiny house. I felt my heartbeat in my skull as I raced closer.

"Stop right there!"

I was met with a rifle pointed at my face and I froze. I watched helplessly as six armed agents poured into my grandparent's tiny cabin on the edge of Bow Bend Lake. It was the first time today that I noticed the wet November air on my barely-covered skin. The eyes of the agent in front of me never waivered until I felt Jack's hand on my shoulder.

"It's okay, he's with me," Jack motioned for me to follow.

We finished crossing the short distance in silence and I braced myself for the worst. I took Jack's somber face as a sign that what I would see in that cabin would be my every fear come to life. Swallowing hard, I stepped with him onto the porch and as I looked up, Charlie came into the doorway.

I saw she was fighting against anger as she moved toward us. Handing Jack her firearm, she wrapped her arms around my waist and I pulled her into me.

"I killed her...I didn't want to. She left me no choice," she finally whispered.

Jack looked from me to Charlie, "She was going to kill you. You did what you had to do."

"I know."

He raised his chin at me and, turning with Charlie still in my arms, we slowly returned to the command center.

CHAPTER SIXTY-SIX

CHARLIE

Killing an old high school friend, even a deranged, murderous one, was never on my bingo card.

As the days passed, I learned more about Audrey Campbell Dawson than I thought possible. And while she'd murdered one of the last remaining members of my family, I did feel sorry for her. She was sick and in ways that I don't think even those closest to her knew or understood.

She was, however, exceptionally good at hiding her true self. Her husband, Jimmy, owned a small company producing polystyrene foam with his father, Jimmy, Senior. Audrey was known to all the employees as a *"bright and curious woman who wanted to know everything about the business"* which just happened to include how chemicals like pentane were used and stored.

It turns out that Audrey's obsession with me began in the middle of our high school careers. Upon the review of evidence our techs collected at the scene, it was found that she left notes about me next to every picture in each yearbook. They began innocently enough with words like "Best Friends Forever" and the acronym "LYLAS", *love you like a sister*, scrolled in her cute looping handwriting with its heart-dotted I's. But, as the years progressed, her delusions deepened and the lighthearted terms of endearment turned dark. My senior picture was blacked out with marker and with the word "whore" written in block letters along its edge. Words like "traitor", "slut", and "bitch" followed.

Several journals were found among the stockpile of personal items. Most of them were decades old and revealed the state of mind of my old classmate, but the newest ones were like reading transcripts from her confessional. The earliest was dated almost two decades ago and right around the time she started sleeping with my ex-husband.

Audrey wrote: *"I will never understand what my Dearest sees in the likes of Davy Wyatt. He's crude, barely literate, and completely without a soul. My Dearest can do so much better than that gorilla. I will show my Dearest that they are special. They are worth far more than rubies."*

She continued to refer to me as her Dearest throughout the thousands of pages of prose over the years. She admitted to sleeping with Davy as a way to prove to me that he was unfaithful by nature and that my catching them had been a mistake.

In the more recent passages, she described how very hurt she was that I didn't spend more time with her at the reunion and that it would be the last time I, or anyone else, ignored her. She left the hotel shortly after we ran into each other and on impulse, decided to burn down the church where we grew up.

The same place where *"My Dearest took her oath of purity with me and where she lied to God"*.

She didn't realize Nettie would be in the sanctuary so late at night and when my aunt questioned her motives for being there, she hit her over the head with a statue. After the fire was set, she had a difficult time removing my aunt from the building, so she left her near the door and called 911.

She never intended for Nettie to get hurt and it was the only thing she expressed any guilt over.

After the first blaze, Audrey found the experience of fire exciting and in some respects, cleansing. It was her first taste of catharsis, no matter how demented it seemed, she felt vindicated.

After realizing Eric left the Falls, she followed him back to Las Vegas under the guise of a business trip. She stalked Eric for several days only to realize that he already had someone watching him. She wrote that Marta was sick with a *"desperate and unhealthy love"* for Eric, and she wanted to protect him from her and me because he was *"a decent human."* The writings continued to place her in Seattle and Portland at the time of those fires as well. The lines of prose were reckless and violent. She wrote that out of every person in the world, I was the vilest because I was a fraud, and could hide among good people, like a *"cobra in a rice field"*.

Additional to the journals and among the piles of other memorabilia, were notebooks of unsent love letters to Davy and Eric, pictures of me with her face superimposed over mine, rejection letters from the Portland police academy, a motorcycle license, and a variety of paper targets from a local shooting range. Out of the many curious bits was a tiny gold ring made with a small setting of a sparkling turquoise-colored stone. It was the traditional color for those born in December, like me. While sifting through the piles of tagged evidence, I set my eyes on the simple ring, and along with it, a memory flashed in my mind.

Two girls, both thirteen stood with several others at the front of a full sanctuary on Sunday morning. A man in a dark suit and tie smiled down at them from his pulpit while preaching about the Virgin Mary and wholesomeness. The girls looked at each other, their eyes full of hope and promise, holding tiny circles of gold in their right palms. After a few more words from the pastor, the entire group of teens took their rings and placed them on the ring finger of their left hands. Joyous piano music played...

I would never know how Audrey got her hands on my ring or even when or how I lost track of it all those years ago. What was certain was that I hadn't given it to her and that trinket meant more to her than it did to me. But, apparently, *I* meant more to Audrey than anyone knew. I would never presume to say the woman was in love with me, although the evidence certainly pointed in that direction but I would go as far as to say she had an unhealthy obsession for an ideal that could never be.

One of the most intriguing pieces of everything found in the cabin was an employee badge for Hulker-Merriem labs in Las

Vegas, Nevada in the name of Marta Di Luca. As it turns out, before Marta took her own life, she was a lab technician for a company that commonly used pentane in its distillation of essential oils. During the bureau's investigation, it was learned that Hulker-Merriem's accounting department reported a discrepancy in its inventory numbers for its stock of pentane, but because it was thought to be a problem with their ordering and not the real count, no red flags were raised. It was surmised that because she couldn't just carry a flammable liquid on a plane with her, she used Marta's identification to get it herself.

Jack and I suspect she may have had something to do with the death of Marta, but with no evidence otherwise, we've been forced to sit on those suspicions.

The FBI questioned her husband about her activities over the past several months. It was determined that he had no cause for concern or to even suspect his wife of any criminal conduct. In his words, he described her as, "An angel who loved flowers and would move mountains for the people she loved."

Part of me felt guilty for my role in her mental decline. I didn't know and couldn't remember how or when we stopped being friends all those years ago, I just knew I must have played some part that she could never get over or forgive. But, even when confronted with facts of the events, she just couldn't face her own mistakes or the truth.

Those in the field of psychology would call it a type of extreme cognitive dissonance. Audrey believed she was in love with me, or the idea of me, while simultaneously hating me because she thought I abandoned her and the promise we made as children. She tried to balance and rationalize her feelings for decades until it was just too much and her internal anger took control. Her mental decline may have driven her to madness, but the truth pushed her over the edge of the cliff.

I was back to full duty within a few days of the incident at the cabin with another clean shoot in my jacket. I used my days off to check in with Josie and thank Chief Herandez for his watchful eye over my cousin. Before a drive to Portland to catch my plane to Seattle, I made a small detour through the cemetery to Nettie's grave.

My cold hands fumbled with the small bouquet of red roses, "Hey, Nettie. I...uhh...I'm so sorry for...everything. I miss you so much and I know I don't have a right to. It's my fault...I know that, for not...you know, being around. I promise I won't let Josie down. I'll make you proud."

"You already do," a deep voice spoke, its tone sending familiar and pleasing chills down my spine.

Looking over my shoulder, I smiled, "What are you doing here?"

"I thought I might find you," Eric approached, wrapping his arm around my waist. "How *are* you?"

I nodded, laying the flowers on my aunt's headstone, "I'm...okay. Ready to get back to a normal life...I mean, as normal as it can be."

Turning around, we walked toward the narrow, paved driving path of the cemetery. The gray clouds billowed overhead and the air smelled heavy with ozone; it would start raining soon. I popped the collar of my coat to keep the damp, November chill off my neck before linking my arm with Eric's.

"Does that normal life still involve me?" he looked down at our entwined arms. I stopped on the path, facing him.

"Why would you think it wouldn't?"

He chortled and smiled softly, "I'm just making sure nothing's changed for you."

"We've got some details to work out...but, I know I want to be with you and a little distance isn't going to stop me," I smiled back.

"In that case, I have an offer to make," moving closer, he brushed the wind-whipped hair from my face with his finger.

I cut him a sly grin, "I'm listening."

"Come home with me."

"What?" I furrowed my brow.

"You heard me. I want you to come home with me," his deep green eyes sparkled in the muted light.

"Eric, I have a career...you said you could handle this...me...everything. I'm not leaving the bureau—"

His warm lips stopped me mid-sentence and while it infuriated me, it also turned me on.

"I'm not asking you to leave," he replied quickly as he pulled away. "Commute...use ESP...transfer if you want. But I don't want to live another moment without you or another night without you against me."

Nothing I could have said would have been the right words at that moment so I said the only thing that felt natural, "Are you sure?"

Leaning down, his tongue danced with mine. The heat from his body pulsed with every tender movement of his mouth, making my insides throb. Raindrops gently fell as we ignored the world around us. The droplets turned into gentle waves of cold rain as we continued to kiss and in a matter of seconds, we were completely soaked.

Eric finally pulled away, purring in my ear, "Let's go home."

EPILOGUE

Chapter Sixty-Seven

ERIC

I watched her face contort in anguish. I knew she was in excruciating pain but there wasn't a damn thing I could do to stop or ease it. It killed me that I couldn't trade places with her for even a second, but I was only the support system. I also knew it wouldn't last forever, she and I would get through this.

Holding on to her hand, I allowed her fingernails to dig into the flesh of my palm, "You're doing great, baby! You can do this, Charlie."

I kept my voice smooth and calm as I soothed her.

"Oh my God! You fucking suck at this," she growled mid-groan. The blonde woman in dark green smiled at me as she took Charlie's pulse. She seemed very comfortable with angry women insulting their partners.

"Remember to breathe, Charlie," she instructed mildly.

"Why don't you breathe!" Charlie bit back as I saw the tiniest bit of relief pass over her face. "I'm sorry...I didn't mean—"

The young woman smiled again, "It's okay...I get it, I do. But, Charlie...you *can* do this. It won't be long."

She left the room. Part of me wanted her to stay because Charlie was a formidable woman. She knew how to turn a three-hundred-pound man into a sobbing mess and she could use a gun. Extremely well and with deadly accuracy. Was I a little afraid of her right now?

Yes, without a doubt and I am secure enough to admit that.

With every sear of pain, she blamed me. Was it my fault? Well, the short answer is yes but, as they say, it takes two to tango. Charlie and I tangoed a lot and we are exceptionally good at it.

Turning back to her, I saw anxiety and worry fill her face. It was a look I wasn't expecting and I didn't like to see.

"What's the matter," I kissed her hand still entangled in mine.

She took a deep breath, "I'm sorry, Eric...for everything I've said in the last few hours. I don't mean any of it. You know...I can't do any of this without you."

Kissing her hand again, I smiled, "I love you with every piece of my soul, Charlotte Tilset. From the moment you walked into that ballroom, I knew my life would finally begin. There is no me without you."

She giggled.

"What's so funny?" I squeezed her hand.

"I've been Hanson for so long, it's weird to hear Tilset," her hazel eyes glowed.

I pursed my lips teasingly, "You can change it back if you want. I mean, we just dropped the license off a few days ago."

"Not in a million years!" Her laughter filled the room until it turned into a bellow of pain. "Eric! Where's that doctor!?"

"What do you need, Charlie?" Now I was starting to panic.

"I need to push!"

Chapter Sixty-Eight

CHARLIE

My son slept peacefully in my arms. I have never seen anything or anyone more beautiful in my life and I know whatever magic made him could only be outdone by the enchantment that created his twin brother.

I am a mom of twins.

I never imagined my life turning out the way it has. A year and a half ago, I was just an FBI Special Agent; one of fourteen thousand across the entire organization. I arrested bad guys and drank even worse coffee, and I thought that my life had all the meaning it needed in doing what little I could to make the world a safer place.

I ran into Eric and my perspective changed. I found a real partner in life that I can count on to have my back. He is gorgeous, smart, and sexy as hell. I still berate myself for taking so damn long to fall in love, but when I did, I fell hard. He makes me feel respected, safe, and complete. He was the missing piece I had no idea I was missing.

After the shooting at the cabin, Eric and I decided we were no longer satisfied with seeing how things went. If a threat to you or the one that you love teaches you anything, it's that life is just too fucking short. We weren't going to waste a single minute waiting around.

We moved in together quite literally the next day and it was the best decision we have made. Being back in Portland meant shuttle flights home every weekend from Seattle, but it gave me a real place to come home to. It also meant I could finally be the guardian I needed to be for Josie, who was over the moon with my new living situation.

Living together also meant there was very little Eric and I could keep from each other, so there were no secrets. Every single detail of our lives was out in the open and on display for the other to see. Something completely new for both of us.

When I was sick for a solid week right at the New Year, Eric came home early with a bag from the pharmacy. He nervously handed me the box inside, as I lay on the sofa eating saltine crackers.

"What's this?" I took it from him, noticing he was searching for the right words.

"I think," he paused. "I think you should take that test."

It was then I turned over the box, realizing he handed me a home pregnancy kit. I looked at him amused.

"Eric, I'm not pregnant. I've got the flu. Jack was sick last week...it's been going around—"

He cut me short, kneeling beside me, "Charlie. Let's be adults...when was your last period? Because...we've been together nearly every night since before Thanksgiving and...well..." he shrugged. "And we haven't been exactly practicing safe sex."

It was true. We were like horny teenagers most nights and birth control be damned.

I humored him, never really thinking the test would come out positive. So, when it did, I made him go buy another. When that one was positive too, we cried together. Not out of embarrassment or devastation, but out of excitement and joy. The meaning we thought we found in our careers and each other was minuscule compared to that moment. We made something out of love together and we began jokingly calling the child our "home improvement" project.

As I came into my second trimester, I requested desk duty, and lucky for me, DSAC Covey was willing to oblige. Bart didn't want me off his team so with me asking for an administrative assignment, it allowed him to keep me, Jack, and Emile together, once Emile finally returned to the bureau with a clean bill of health. Of course, that was until last month when I started my maternity leave for the next twelve weeks. Flying even for an hour was getting to be a hassle and the commute was now strongly against my doctor's advice.

My team will be fine, I think; as long as they don't touch my desk.

It was last Thursday night as Eric and I sat cuddled on our sofa when our lives altered once more. I lay leaned against Eric's broad chest as he rubbed my exhausted shoulders, Pip curled between my legs, and our babies doing what felt like cartwheels in my swollen abdomen.

I groaned, "That feels so good...I don't know why, but I'm just drained tonight."

"I'm betting being thirty-five weeks pregnant with twins has something to do with it," he continued to massage my neck, laughing.

"I wish they would just sleep right now...I'm starting to feel like I'm on a carnival ride with as much as they are playing in there," I rubbed my hands over my bulging and firm belly.

"Boys. Be good to your mother," he commanded in his best *Dad* voice.

The sensation in my womb settled.

Craning my neck to look at him, I winked, "Nice job, Tilset."

With the children-induced nausea finally calmed, I leaned further into Eric's hard chest. My eyes were drowsy and were just starting to droop when his baritone whispered in my ear.

"I have something I want to ask you."

"Mmm..hmm," was my quiet response and I felt him reach into the pocket of his shorts.

"I love you more than life itself, Charlotte Hanson. You've given me so much in this life already...I mean...you're making me a father. Something, I thought I'd missed my chance at being. But, I have one more request," the rhythm of his inflection and the feel of his breath on my ear sent chills down my spine.

"I'm listening," I purred, eyes still closed.

"Will you marry me?"

I immediately felt like the wind was knocked from my chest and my eyes flew open to find, in his outstretched hand, a diamond engagement and wedding ring in a velvety maroon box. I was rendered speechless. Marriage was something we thought about, sure, but it was a down-the-road discussion. A *we'll-think-about-it-in-a-year-or -two* talk. Something we tabled for another time.

I felt in his chest that he was holding his breath.

My answer was quick and confident, "Yes! Yes, I will marry you!"

After taking a few minutes to roll my dump truck-sized body to a sitting position, Eric tried to slide the engagement ring on my breakfast link-sized finger. The ring didn't fit like it should have, so he put the magnificent piece on my pinky. We rolled with laughter until we both had tears streaming down our faces at the comedy of it all. Once we were able to get a full sentence out without cracking, we decided that waiting was again something we refused to do.

Early the next morning, after making a quick detour at a jewelry store so I could purchase a band for him, we were at the county clerk's office to apply for our license. Once the elderly woman with smiling eyes heard our reasons for wanting to marry quickly, she was more than happy to waive our three-day waiting period. I'd like to think it was the story of our love affair and not that I looked like I might give birth at any minute on the beautiful antique marble tile that was the persuading factor. After which, we took a romantic elevator ride to the third floor to meet with a friend of mine, the honorable Joelle Renaud, to perform the ceremony. Then, it was back to the clerk to file the paperwork.

That was three days ago.

Tonight, as I cradled Declan in my arms, I felt my world filling with hope where, eighteen months ago, I only felt doubt. I lost so much in my life but, in this exquisite moment, I was sure all the heartache had a driving purpose to get me here.

"Ready to trade?" Eric whispered. "I think Jasper's hungry."

"I can do that," I gave him a wry smile, "Just means you're on diaper duty."

About the Author

January Kelly is a longtime writer and holds a BS in Sociology with an interest in Religious Studies. She is an avid reader of fantasy and science fiction and a lover of all genres of music. January is based in the wilds of the Missouri Midwest where she loves to embroider bad words on bookmarks, have cocktails and queso with her friends, and go on long walks with her husband, Jarritt.

www.januarykelly.com

Follow on Facebook:

https://www.facebook.com/profile.php?id=10006785073041
5

Instagram:

https://www.instagram.com/januarykelly.author/?next=%2F

www.januarykelly.com

Follow on Facebook:

https://www.facebook.com/profile.php?id=100067850730415

Instagram:

https://www.instagram.com/januarykelly.author/?next=%2F